TEMPEST OF FAE

These Hallowed Hills 7

Quick Quill Publishing, LLC © 2022

Also by S.L. Mason

THESE HALLOWED HILLS

TRICK OF FAE

TEST OF FAE

THORNS OF FAE

TWIST OF FAE

TRAITS OF FAE

THIEF OF FAE

TEMPEST OF FAE

DEDICATION

To my brother Tim and his wife, my found sister, Esther.

You sheltered me when I was in a storm. I can never repay

your kindness only offer these feeble words,

Thank you

Spell/Song List

New Magic

Tears for Fears – *Shout*

Disturbed - *The Sound of Silence*

Big Bad Voodoo Daddy's - *Hey, Lou*

Annie Lenox - *It feels like walking on broken glass*

Queen - *Who wants to live forever*

Planet Soul – *Set you free*

Selena Gomez - *Slow down*

Queen – *We will rock you*

Wolfshiem - *I Find You're Gone*

The Commodores - *Brick House*

Huey Lewis & The News - *Back in time*

Harry Nilsson - *A lime in the coconut*

Baha Men - *Who let the dogs out*

Old Magic

Jack be nimble

Ring around the roses

Sixpence

My Jack in the box

Humpty Dumpty

The worms go in, the worms go out

The old man is snoring

A wise old owl

TABLE OF CONTENTS

CHAPTER 1

MERCIA

She was terrific. Her black hair flowed behind her while her thorny white crown reached for the sky. Her golden eyes burned like a solar flare, ripping into my soul, tearing me down to the very bones that made me. The green wings heaved with her breathing, slow and steady. All the stories of wings were wrong. They weren't pretty. They inflicted terror, a terror I'd felt so rarely, making the taste foreign.

Magic moves with intent, and wings can push that intent to the edge of oblivion with one powerful beat.

That wasn't what scared me. No, it was her clarity of understanding. Her eyes spoke of everything she'd ever lived, and they dared you to defy her. On a level most creatures never could, she got it - the fight, the hunger for the hunt, and everything that came with it. I could see it. She was just like me - a killer to the core.

I swallowed back the waking fear that laced my bones. She may be Queen, but my father and mother stood up to her.

I, too, will stand. She will hear reason.

At least, that's what I hoped.

I wanted to bite my lip and hold back all that was bursting to be heard, but *they* were watching - the Fae.

I preferred humanity. They were easy to anticipate. Their choices were driven by their needs.

Fae didn't work that way. The wheels within wheels turned at all times in the Hallowed Hills. There was never just one front to fight on, yet the fight came from all sides at all times.

Momma said never to turn your back on any Fae. I couldn't imagine how she ever caught a wink of sleep here.

I wanted to glance at Puca. That was a tale of its own. I would not show my hand before my time. Patience was the necessary quality of a hunter.

We must be willing to hold a position until the perfect moment of attack.

Puca lingered on the edge of Fae society, watching and waiting.

For what? For his moment?

I didn't know if the Fae knew who I was, but they knew what I was - a changeling, a halfbreed, a hunter. They were all waiting to see what the Queen would do with me - kill me for being Pil's child or embrace me for being the last remaining vestige of Arthur.

Arty, dear old dad, a man I never met.

None of that mattered really.

Hug me, fight me, whatever floats your boat.

Puca made me swear, and I was his weapon, just like my mother. I was her child in every way. I would fight and kill to end this Human/Fae war and free everyone I cared about. Nothing and no one would stand in my way. Not even the Queen.

Dear old dad's best friend.

"Kneel before your souvenir." Her voice rang, and the walls shivered with the decree, making the leaves dry and shrink.

I didn't. Instead, I lifted my head and stared her down.

Her eyes softened as I looked up at her through the hair hanging in my face. She quickly shut whatever she was thinking down. Like curtains in a window, the feelings were closed off away from the world.

"Do it!" She growled. The wakes of her charisma hit like a steel ball shot from an old-style gun. My knees met the floor with a painful crack.

With great difficulty, I pulled my head up to glare at her and gritted my teeth.

"I know where Nick and Janice are being held," I spat.

Most of the room gasped. The sycophants clutched their pearls and covered their mouths.

"In Lanta. Wherever that is," she replied.

A devilish smile scraped across my face as it revealed she didn't know everything.

"Release me!" I said without asking. There was no implied *please* or *thank you*. None of that surface crap.

These are my kind. They don't beg or plead.

I wouldn't either.

"Why should I? I can find Lanta on my own," she snapped. The wakes around her ached to scratch my eyes out.

Alice laid a hand on the Queen's shoulder. She never turned her head or batted an eyelash.

"You hunters are all the same, always acting as if the rules of Fae don't apply to you. Pil apparently didn't teach you manners," she remarked.

I growled to release my frustration. This wasn't one of the many scenarios I'd run through my head. I had to reformulate my plan.

I closed my eyes and pushed with all my magical might to stand. The Queen rolled her eyes and raised her hand, ready to push me down.

Before she could hum the spell and smash me to the floor, I ripped a portal into the air next to me. On the other side, there was the rocky face of a mountain with men riding horses etched into the side.

"Momma called that *stone mountain*. It's close to Lanta — Atlanta. On the outskirts of the city is a place run by the Govs called CDC— "

"The CDC?" She asked in a quiet, controlled voice. "You've been there?"

"Yes. It's a fortress, and most of it is underground," I retorted.

The need to jump through the portal grew stronger with every second I kept it open. Yet, I closed my hand, slamming the portal shut.

"How can you open a portal?" She demanded.

"They are harvesting Fae bone marrow and injecting it into humans," I growled.

Sarinha blanched.

"Janice," she whispered.

I nodded my head, "And Nick. They are going to bleed them dry to build an army." I didn't bother to explain anymore.

Everyone can just connect the dots for themselves.

We didn't have time to hold hands and lead people down the primrose path.

The Queen pulled a portal open and pointed. "Go, protect that boy." Alice stepped through the opening and disappeared.

The Queen took to her feet, her wings doing most of the work.

"Every Fae in this room not sworn to Puca or me will never leave."

A chuckle rang from a far-off corner along with the flash of canary-colored eyes. The dark hair rippled in waves back from the face of perfection. Puca Oberon was enjoying the show.

I caught his eye. He winked at me and crooked a finger my way.

Internally, I groaned. The last thing I wanted to do was have a convo with my master and one-time King of Fae. He would have a request, which was really his way of giving me a quest, and the magic would force me to obey.

But I couldn't stop the magic that pushed me toward my destiny. My feet moved of their own accord, and I didn't fight the motion. I only hoped to find an answer on the other side of the room.

As I moved, the doors to the room slammed shut, and half of the occupants fell to their knees in obedience.

The Queen was speaking, but I couldn't hear her, nor could I obey. The power of her magic couldn't override the power of my oath.

Magic has its rules, and the oath apparently beat out a Queen.

Her voice droned on in the background. Most of what she was saying wasn't directed at me. I barely noticed the sound of sniveling and death. Warm flecks of blood splattered the side of my face. I wiped them away and glanced back at the Queen.

She held a gun in one hand and a quicksilver sword in the other. A female Fae knelt at her feet. The Queen's lips moved, and the female replied.

I snapped back to the reality of the situation.

"Mercia?" Puca inquired.

I blinked and whipped to face him. "Yes, master?"

The sound of the Queen's voice overwrote whatever she was going to say, and I instinctively turned to listen.

"Swear your allegiance to me and Fae, or die!" Her voice was cool and controlled.

The Fae replied, "I will never swear to a Seelie Queen." The female at her feet spit, and before the spittle could reach the floor, her head was gone. It landed on the floor with a hollow ring. Melons give off the same sound when you drop them on the ground.

I swallowed back the vitriol that rose. But the hunter in me overwrote that human response and smirked. That Fae chose poorly.

She'd at least have a chance at life if she'd sworn.

The line of Fae behind her was longer than I realized. Why hadn't she cemented her rule sooner?

Puca gripped the meat of my shoulder, and my attention returned to my master.

"The CDC is a death trap," he remarked, then shivered like the coat on a horse.

"So was New Orleans, and look how that turned out," I replied. The smirk I carried for the Queen never left my face, and for a moment, I didn't feel the fear of losing.

"Arrogance is what brought all this on. Don't follow down that path. Jacques, too, believed he and Jillian were unbeatable. Look where that brought us. Magic must have balance."

The smirk drained away.

Momma said overconfidence is the hunter's downfall.

"Forget about the CDC. There is one last thing you must retrieve." Puca's golden eyes turned the color of a poppy. "Where is the grimoire?"

I don't know.

But I couldn't tell Puca that. Puca didn't suffer defeat, and neither could I. Not again. What would I lose this time? Nick, Ron, Fadmor, and all the kids?

"Master—" I faltered.

"I don't want to hear it. You know what hangs in the balance. Don't come back without it!" He growled.

The hair on my body shivered, and I stood up. I gave him a curt nod and opened my hand to tear open a portal. A second later, I was kissing the stone wall.

"You will not escape this room without my leave!" Sarinha roared. She was behind me, breathing over my shoulder. "I see you," she whispered. Her voice reminded me of a cross between Nick and Puca with a dash of Alice. All rolled into a terrifying burrito of power folded around me.

"Where were you sending her?"

"She is the only clue to what we seek," Puca replied, as a matter of factly. The shuffling of feet filled the air around us. Puca was eager to send me on my way.

"She is not your subject to command," Sarinha replied.

"She doesn't answer to you either. She, like myself and Nick, is outside your control. How do you think she's been able to travel between the realms? Let her go!" Now he was whispering.

The wakes from a portal tore the wall next to me, and I was plucked by my jacket off the wall, the magic pulling me through.

CHAPTER 2

SARAH

The way her hair hung in her face made her look just like Arty, only without the glasses. A rock momentarily lodged in my throat.

I poured those emotions into a little bottle and locked them away in the cabinet marked as *'shit for later.'*

I grabbed the back of her coat and drug her into a chamber away from the prying eyes of Fae, and all the scheming.

Puca stepped through before I could close the portal in his face.

I heaved a sigh of irritation.

"Can I not have a moment to speak to her?" I demanded. The girl hadn't even squeaked when I tossed her on the floor.

In my mind, she was a kid. But in actual age, we were more or less the same.

"Do you think Jacques is taking time for a tete with old friends?" Puca rejoined, slicking his hair back, and giving the girl a wink.

I turned to the look. Arty's eyes stared at me out of this girl's face. "Mercia? Is that it?" I asked to cover the churned-up feelings just from looking at her.

She snapped to her feet, "That is what my mother named me," was the tart reply.

I wanted to smile. Arty would have pointed out the obvious too. But I didn't. I couldn't. That Sarah died with Arty and everything else that was good in my life.

Other than Janice.

"Lanta is Atlanta?" I remarked.

"I said that," she replied and glared at me like I was wasting her time. Her eyebrows held high. She was waiting for me to say or do something.

"What's your plan?" I just wanted her to do something normal. It was dumb. She wasn't normal, and I could see it. Her Fae markings were intertwined with two colors. No one I'd seen carried marking like that. They were two shades of green, of which one was moss green.

Just like Nick's.

"They gave you Nicks marrow, didn't they," I stated.

Her blue eyes hardened as she clenched her jaw and ground out, "Yes. Before he changed into a wolf."

I gasped and whipped my head around to gaze at Puca. He tilted his head in assurance, signalizing she wasn't lying.

"Are we done here? I have a hunt, and my boyfriend is being used to fuel an evil army. So, I'd like to go if you don't mind," she huffed, using the release of air to puff the hair out of her eyes. "I got people who need killing. Jacques is top of the tower for that one."

A laugh burst from my chest. I couldn't help it. I couldn't remember the last time someone sassed me like that. Other than Puca, and he just rubbed me wrong. And he did it because he could.

That wasn't true. I could remember. It was either Nick or Arty. It didn't matter.

"Where do you think the blanky is?" I asked and crossed my arms.

"The blanky, as you call it, well, I haven't got a clue."

"My mom said that last she saw it was right after you were born, in a duffel bag Pil carried."

"Momma and I lost that bag in a building collapse. When she died." Mercia's matter-of-fact reply hurt me. Her mother died, and she didn't flinch as she said it.

I was starting to think I wasn't playing poker as well as she did. I always felt like they could see me sweating. She, on the other hand, was a cold rock standing in a river bed, unmoving.

"Where did she die?"

"A city I can't return to." She tore her hard eyes away from me. She wasn't sad. She was just staring at Puca.

He acted as if he didn't notice her inquiring gaze. Yet even I felt the way her eyes were peeling back every layer of skin on his body.

"Why can't you go back?" I finally broke the tension and asked.

Puca shuffled around the two of us, and Mercia moved with him. She side-eyed me, "Because I don't know where it was," she replied.

Puca stopped his dancing. The indifferent facial expressions changed to surprise. "What do you mean? You were there! Pill called me. How could you not know where you were?" He demanded.

She shrugged, "I was only two years out of my chrysalis. We passed through many cities before Momma died. Sometimes she traveled with me asleep on her back."

I pulled in a deep breath.

Pil, you fucking bitch! You fought with a baby on your back!?

Puca didn't seem as concerned as I was over dragging a baby into battle.

I wanted to ask more, but there was no longer a human side left in me. That innate curiosity that so marks humanity just wasn't there anymore. The only driving force I felt was for the hunt and win.

Not like Mercia. She waked with the vestiges of her humanity. There wasn't much, but enough to still claim she had some.

I didn't have a drop. Even my hair was fully Fae. When I looked in the mirror, all I saw was my Fae wakes pulsing back at me. Whatever humanity I'd been born with burned away with the stone throne.

Mercia's wakes were strong, yet her humanity lined her magic. It wasn't gone, only fading.

She glanced at me, "I was never a child, not like you think. I was born Fae, the size of a ten-year-old child or thereabouts. Whatever ideas you have about my mother are wrong. We are Fae, you and I. Humanity was a thin veneer we hid behind, a glamor." She arched her eyebrow at me.

I wasn't sure if it was bait or a question. Either way, the silence was a better way to find my answers.

"So, when you opened the portal in the throne room, where were you going? Shanghai?" He demanded, with his eyes the color of a glowing ember.

She actually swallowed.

Interesting. She fears Puca and not me.

"I was going to find Nick because he would know the city where Momma died," she spat. Everything about her changed. The wakes took on the edge of a knife, and her eyes glowed at the challenge issued by Puca.

"Pull back, Mercia, or I will tear you to shreds where you stand. And where would that leave Nick?" a low growl burst from Puca's chest, vibrating the air.

It tickled the hair in my nose.

"Enough! This tete is over. Oberon, Mercia, it looks like you are stuck with each other. Puca, take her to the woobie and secure it from Jacques!" I ordered.

Both heads whipped in my direction. The red coals in their face burned with anger.

"You forget yourself, Sarinha!" Puca growled, saliva dripping from a long canine.

"No, I don't. This is the solution. You've been there. Therefore, you can take her there. If you need to whip out your dick to prove something, please don't. I don't care."

"She's right." Mercia stated, "That is the best solution. You need only open a portal. I will do the rest." She relaxed back into her stance. Her arms were still loose at her sides, yet close to a weapon.

I'd only just realized that the bumps and folds in her clothing were filled with weapons of all varieties. She was a walking arsenal.

Between the long rifle on her back and the crossbow hanging under her arm, you would think she was weight down, but her back was as straight as an arrow.

She had finger daggers all over her chest, almost like armor. Everything was angled according to a left or right-hand pull. She had the most advantageous placement for each and every tool in her arsenal. I quickly memorized the layout for my own purposes. The leather bodice would come in handy when I went to kill Jacques.

Mercia didn't budge. She glared at me. "You aren't what I pictured."

I stared her down, "What did you think? That I was a fairy Queen and would give you a flower necklace to show off to your friends?" I retorted. My wings flared.

This was the first time anyone said I didn't meet their expectations. That really chapped my hide.

She hitched her lips to one side, "No way. I just expected something else. Momma never spoke of you or my dad." She turned away from me as if that was the end of the conversation.

"You look like him, like Arty. Only he had glasses." It was all I could give. If I said another word, the rock in the throat would find its way to my belly, and the walls would run with my tears.

She smiled, "Yeah, humans have bad eyes. I guess I got mine from Momma." She winked.

"If you are both done, it's time to go," Puca broke in. His dancing around the room had turned into a shuffle and a tap.

He would have made a great dancer at the Met in New York.

If the Met still existed.

Puca tore a portal into the wall, tilted his head at me, and he and Mercia stepped through it. I couldn't tell where they went, but there was a ton of rubble there.

CHAPTER 3

MERCIA

Sarah never even smiled at me. I didn't expect much. So, I wasn't disappointed.

If I was younger, the scene before me could have resembled the chaos from another time. Instead, it was the world I was born into—the world after the fall. Large chunks of cement created a pile of rubble blanketed in moss. Grass grew up between the cracks, and tree roots snaked over sections. The leftover bits of copper from the building were covered in the green patina of age. Yet, iron waked nearby, and the heat from it barely burned me.

"Where are we?" I asked through gritted teeth.

"How should I know? This was the building," Puca supplied and waved his hands around to indicate the various piles of fake rock.

I stared at the surrounding area. Other than iron that dotted the area, waking its deadly poison, nothing of power leaped out at me.

"Do you see anything?" I asked, then swallowed. No tears pricked my eyes, but an ache I thought I had put to bed long ago pushed at my chest.

Puca didn't reply. His feet danced over rock and mortar until the familiar outline of re-bar sticking out of a chunk of concrete came into view. He squatted down and ran a finger across the moss covering the location of Momma's last breath.

He turned his head to take me in, "There's nothing left. Good." He took to his feet and paced the area, stepping over rocks and bushes.

The small part of me that was human wanted to touch the ground where Momma died, to scour the area for even a hair fiber. A lump formed. This was pointless. I didn't need any hair like some human mutt. I needed to finish this quest and find Nick.

"The fire of Fae destroys everything," Puca remarked without looking back at me. Instead, he kicked a rock that skittered across a flat section of ground before hitting a clump of grass and coming to a stop.

"What does the grimoire look like?" I ventured. The world after the fall didn't have things like quilts. Ratty blankets and bits of clothes sewn together to make a covering, yes. But a quilt with rhyme or reason and magic, no.

"I've not seen it in some time. It was a mixture of earthen colors, as befits something made by a Fae. Each square was unique to the witch that formed it, each generation contributing to the overall pattern," he shrugged, tapped a finger to his lips, and whorled around on one foot with the other leg bent and his arms straight up in the air.

It was magical, and I could see how humans would find him entrancing without charisma. He was indeed a dangerous fantasy to which one couldn't easily turn away from.

The vision of Nick smiling at me on the bridge jump flooded my mind. The moss green of his eyes spoke of flirting and desire. I used that memory to push Puca's charisma away.

His answer was a non-answer. I hitched my mouth to one side in the hope that answers would come to me. Nothing did. The blanket wasn't there.

It may never have been here.

I didn't think it was in the cave with us when I emerged from my chrysalis. Momma carried a duffel bag for all the years of my life with her. I sat down next to the block she died on and tried to think.

Where was the last place I saw it?

If there was anything left of Momma, it would surely be here and willing to help me.

Wouldn't it?

Momma and I first went to Lanta looking for Major Willis. He was harvesting the bodies of dead children. Not only that, but he led the group that killed my father.

We couldn't find him anywhere. Then we heard a rumor of Govs attacking other places on the eastern seaboard. So, we followed the gossip and the trail of bodies and bones. Other than crossing an ocean, the bag was never gone from her side.

She never opened it, and I never asked what she was carrying. It was one of the many things Momma never spoke of.

Now, I wish I had a small dose of human curiosity.

I would have asked and maybe paid more attention. I would have opened it while Momma wasn't looking, and I'd had some idea what I was looking for.

I closed my eyes to replay the last few scenes in my mind.

When my eyes popped open, I realized that the bag was never there

"We are in the wrong city," I stated and took to my feet. "We have to be." I glanced around the rubble. There was nothing. Yet my certainty never wavered.

"Perhaps you are correct. Pil would not have left the safety of the grimoire to chance." Puca shivered in his equine fashion, then turned his head this way and that. His eyes darted around the area, smacked his hands, and rubbed them together.

"Well, I did my part. I brought you to the scene of Pil's death. You are on your own." He opened a portal and moved towards it.

I jumped between him and his magical escape. "I don't think so. I don't have the first clue where I am or where to look. Nick is in Lanta, and every moment we waste looking is a chance he could die!" I shouted. My chest seized with fear.

A brief vision of Nick's body lying on a table lined in iron, gray and bloodless froze my heart.

Puca's horse-like features evaporated, leaving behind nothing but the wolf. His fiery eyes bored into mine and a deep growl rumbled in his chest. "Whose fault is it that Nick is where he is, Hunter?"

I tilted my head down to look at the moss-covered ground exposing my neck. "I should have listened to you, Master," I replied, then swallowed away my pride. "I need your help. I didn't know my mother as well as you did."

It was the only apology I could offer.

I will never say sorry like one of those human mutts.

However, Puca needed me to submit before him, or he wouldn't help.

"Why do you think Pil had the grimoire with her? She was clever. Dragging it around on a hunt would not be clever." He smacked two fingers against my forehead, "Think! What would Pil do? What did she tell you to do if she died?"

The smack didn't cause any pain but humiliation, yes. Puca meant it to shame me. If it were anyone else, I would have ripped their throat out.

He closed the portal and shuffled away from me before leaping over rocks here and there. His dark mood bled away to the place where Puca was dancing again. His side steps, followed by a slide, made tapping noises on the relatively flat cement under his feet.

Puca only dances when things are going his way.

I must have said or done something to make him happy. Most of the buildings around this location lay on the ground. One still stood. It was intact, for the most part. I flashed to the front door and whistled the lock open.

"Did you remember something?" Puca whispered in my ear.

Ignoring the charisma as best I could, I pushed into the building. The vestibule was dusted with leaves and grime. The tiles that once graced the floor and stairs were broken and cracked with age. My attention was never on the floor or the tile. They were a distraction from the iron railing edging the stairs.

Puca hissed at the burning wakes rushing at us. "There is a better way."

"There is," I stepped out of the building and sang, '*Come back, Peter, Come back, Paul*' to close the doors. He opened a portal and stepped through it to the roof.

Most of the roof was flat and circled by what was once an iron railing about one foot high. Today, the railing was missing in large sections. Puca joined me in pushing the chunks over the side. The black metal screeched as they slid down the curved side of the building's roof, leaving behind copper-colored marks in the dark green patina of the roof panels.

I cringed away from the sound and the wakes. The screeching continued until Puca had removed all of the offending iron. I turned at the last of the noise only to be confronted with the answer I was up here for, to begin with.

In the distance was the misshapen framework of a pyramid. Pieces of glass still clung to the apex of the structure. I didn't know what I was looking at, but it mattered.

Nick would know.

He knew about the world from before the fall.

I pointed at the pyramid, "What is that?"

Puca leaned over to meet the angle of my arm. "That? Oh, it's odious. Humanity really should get better architecture. It's some museum."

It suddenly hit me that all the buildings around this area were once connected with the pyramid in the middle.

"What museum?" I asked. I flashed to the only door up here and yanked it open. I rushed down the stairs as fast as I could, putting as much space between me and the railing. I hummed *light as a feather* to ease the groaning in the floor joints and rushed through the nearest archway.

The walls were lined with frames, while the floor was littered with broken pieces of marble. A brass stanchion lay on its side with the base planted in the side of a wall. Broken pieces of plaster littered the floor, revealing the slates behind them and the space between the walls.

A brass plaque labeled the room with a name I couldn't read. I stepped over the rubble, looking for any clue. There, at the base of a statue, was a name - Venus De Milo.

"What did they call this place?" I asked.

Puca kicked chunks of marble across the floor, allowing them to smash into the wall.

I glared up at him.

Noise attracts attention. Attention is bad. Trouble always follows noise.

He was stroking his chin when a smile pulled at the sides of his face, "Ah, the Louvre in Paris."

I gulped. "Paris?" I squeaked. "Momma said to never go to Paris."

Puca cocked an eye at me, "Why do you think *Momma* say that?" He moved around the room, touching frames on the wall with the tip of a finger, curling his nostrils at the rotting canvases in them.

My eyes darted around the room. I had to get out of there. This city was a death zone. The feeling of iron waking nearby only hastened my need to leave. The compulsion in Momma's command warred with the demands of my master.

My feet were making their way to a window on the far side of the building. I had to see proof for myself.

There, in the distance, stood what was left of the iron spire that once dominated the skyline of this city. I whipped around to Puca, "I need to leave this place." My heart was beating in my ears, blocking all else.

His jaw hardened as a fresh layer of fur raced over his body, flowing down his torso. His feet changed as he transformed. The one-time Fae King snapped at me with his canine snout, his fiery eyes blazing with his anger.

I stepped back only to trip over a chuck of rubble on the ground and fell on my butt. A moment later, my head slammed into the floor, Puca's front paws pinning me down. A long rope of saliva broke free from his joules, landing on my cheek and slipping down to my neck.

"You will do as I say. I will not stand for your insolence. Fae cannot survive your failure!" He roared, and his breath blasted in my face.

The taste of fear coated my mouth. My insides quivered as I turned my head to the side, fully exposing my neck. My mind screamed not to submit, to fight back. But Puca was the apex predator of Fae. There was no one stronger. I finally understood why my mother chose him for master and not Jacques.

"Don't make me break you. I can and will to save everyone. No one Fae is more important than the salvation of all. The magic will force you to obey," he informed me as if I didn't know already. I had no choice in this matter.

The shivering in my body stopped, and a terrible itching took over.

Suddenly the pressure of Puca's body disappeared as the Fae took shape before me. His eyes bled back to calm's canary yellow, and a wicked smile scraped over his features.

"Stand, hunter!" He ordered.

I rolled onto my side and pushed up onto my feet. Only I was staring at a set of white paws with black nails. My tongue darted out of my mouth to taste the air.

"This changes many things, little hunter," Puca remarked.

CHAPTER 4

SARAH

What should I do now? Scout out Atlanta or cement my kingdom and somehow raise an army? The chair at my desk called me to sit and relax for a moment and think.

Rest comes last.

My dad said *when you didn't know what to do, don't do anything, hold tight and think it through.*

I knew where Janice and Nick were being held. Jacques was probably there with his blood thieves, lording it over all of Georgia. I rolled my head around on my shoulders to loosen the tight muscles holding it upright. It did little good. The tension would never go away.

We visited Georgia when I was a kid. Dad landed near Atlanta when he came home one year. I didn't remember much, other than the highway going in a circle around the main part of the city.

My ass met the chair, and I huffed. My shoulders hunched over as my face slumped into my hands. I needed to work the problem, and I couldn't.

Janice always helped me, and before him, Arty.

Pressure formed in my chest. Mercia looked just like him. There was no doubt she was Arty's daughter or that she was Fae. Everything about her screamed Fae. The magic that made her, spoke of the hunter she was and the blood of Puca.

I whistled up a mirror. Those same bloodlines flowed through my veins too. We were alike in so many ways—my left-hand burst to life in flame, reminding me of all the subtle differences.

No matter how much I may have in common with anyone, there is no one like me.

"Pouting was never your thing," the Arty in my head remarked. He leaned against the door frame and peeked at me through his hair.

It's not real, no matter how much I wish it were.

"No, it wasn't," I drolled and rolled my eyes. "But I want to pout."

"That is the human in you talking. What does the Fae want?" Arty's shade moved across the room, sat in the center of a large couch, and spread his arms out.

Now I'm just talking to myself, hoping to find answers. That's just sad.

"I know you believe that all of your humanity is gone. But it's not, and they will always war with one another for as long as you live. The only way for you to win against Jacques is to embrace all of you."

For the moment, I wanted to be that 20-something college kid who thought she knew everything. I wanted to eat pizza and study for finals.

"That dream you're reliving doesn't exist. That world is gone, just like me, and if you don't make your move, this one will be too." He released a dry laugh. Arty would have found the humor in it all, somehow.

I jumped to my feet, "Arty, I don't know what to do first. Scout out the CDC, free Janice, and Nick? Wait for Mercia and Puca? Fuck! I don't know!" I groaned and paced the room.

"Why can't you do all of those at once?" He asked, then pointed his index finger at me and pulled the fake trigger.

The vision of Arty evaporated, along with any doubt about what I should do.

"My Queen?"

I jumped. "Lavender, you scared the crap out of me."

She lowered her head to say sorry, and part of me wanted to scream. The Fae inability to apologize or acknowledge wrongdoing was the problem. I wanted to chase down that thought. Instead, I stared her down.

"My Queen, there has been a development," she moved her arm to indicate I should exit the room, which I did.

She led me to the library. I expected her to stop at her work table. But we didn't. She led me deeper into the stacks. The tomes grew darker in color as the light illuminating the room faded away. She pushed a shelf, and it opened into the wall.

I should be surprised, yet I'm not.

Of course, there was a hidden passage in the fairy library. Why wouldn't there be one?

The passage continued on for about a hundred yards before coming to another door. It opened into what I could only describe as a laboratory. There were glass beakers and various electronic devices. Some were familiar, others just as alien as the Fae themselves. The center of the room was a large open space with a curved trough dugout in the floor.

The vision of the stone circle from Puca's garden flashed to my mind. She kept it here. One of the devices looked like an oscilloscope. A xylophone lay on a table along with a triangle and a tuning fork. This was Danu's workroom.

Lavender waved me over to a set of shelves. On the top were the newer-looking books, and as you traveled along with the selves, they grew older until every book resembled an illumination from the Middle Ages.

"She was trying to open a portal," Lavender informed me.

I already know this.

She pointed to some words in the book. The opposite page carried a drawing of the stone circle with waking magic in the center.

"Who knows of this place?" I demanded.

"No one, The Record Keeper brought me here."

The song was on my lips and tongue before I could think. A shielding spell, made from an Imagine Dragons song,

"Everybody wants to be my enemy." The feeling of being alone only grew as I sang to protect this room and the secrets of Fae.

Because everyone right now who doesn't see what I see is my enemy.

Lavender shivered as the last notes drifted away in the room. The reverberation hit the walls and ricocheted in every direction. I waited for the magic to settle into its new form. The walls waked with fresh power. The remnants of an older spell tickled the corners of the room. They clung like Spanish moss and hung loose to wave with the fresh layer.

The old spell carried the canary yellow of Puca's eyes and the golden hue of Danu. She must have laid that spell. I moved close to the hanging strands to inspect them. The ends of the wakes were newly frayed. The spell had only been broken recently.

"Who else was here?" I demanded.

Lavender shook her head and splayed her hands in an effort to show she had nothing to hide.

The room only smelled of Lavender and me, along with the scent of the library.

I moved from one section to another, hoping to find a clue as to who broke the spell. Better yet, did they take anything? But all the limp wakes only glowed with the golden hue that permeated most of Fae. The magic gave me nothing to go on.

The room contained no windows and only one door. It was big enough to work in with a small cot in the corner for rest. The structure of the walls was rough with a mixture of dirt and rock. It was little more than a dugout from the American plains.

A sigh escaped before I could stop it.

I ran a hand down the side of my face, and my wings twitched in time with my heart.

My mind kept returning to the recess in the floor. The shape was familiar. I was drawn to its place on the floor. The rectangle reminded me of something. I paced from one side to the other, counting my steps. The numbers were the same, eight. The short ends were each four steps wide. The curved recess was the only part out of place.

I closed my eyes to push the truth away. I didn't want to believe it.

Without a word, I swept from the room.

"My queen?" Lavender called.

"I'll be right back," I called over my shoulder. My feet took me through the golden path right to the front door of the throne room to stand before the stone block.

I stared at the bane of my life and paced off the perimeter.

Eight steps for the long side and four for the short one.

It was a perfect match.

The walls whispered to me, informing me of all the eyes watching their Queen. They would see the counting and pacing as a weakness.

"Get out!" I ordered. The room emptied in a rush as the compulsion of my magic hurried them. I slammed the doors behind the simpering rabble, and the walls interlaced with the opening, creating a lock.

I sang to the lock of the walls and blocked the windows, turning the throne room into a dead zone.

'Come back, Peter, come back, Paul,' I whispered around the room before settling on the stone throne. The massive stone groaned as it slowly pulled from its seat in the floor, revealing the curve in the base.

The floor of the throne room now looked exactly like Danu's lab. The shape and size were identical. I glanced from the throne to the well and back. They were all part of the same set. Danu hid the stones well. I wasn't even sure Puca knew about this.

Danu was clever. Keeping all the pieces of the portal apart for so long could not have happened without planning of some sort.

I snapped my fingers and slowly lowered my hand to ease the throne back into its seat on the floor.

Jacques was only looking for the wand, the bucket, and the well. Without the throne and the grimoire, he had no hope of using them.

But I can.

CHAPTER 5

MERCIA

I was a dog. Well, perhaps a wolf, like Nick and Puca. I turned my head to the side to look at my master and cuffed.

This changes so many things. Fuck!

I snapped my jaws and growled, then leaped right and back to the left. I whirled around just to feel the motion. The fur on my tail tickled my nose, and I sneezed. I stopped and sat down and yipped.

"Yes, being a wolf can be fun. Turn back and tell me everything you remember after you hatched." Puca sat down on the floor with his legs crossed and his chin in the palm of a hand.

I sat back on my haunches and looked around. I didn't know how I turned to begin with, so how could I change back? I lowered my snout and huffed at Puca.

I needed a clue, and he had one. I knew it.

He rolled his eyes, "I guess the first time is always the hardest. You have to want to do something human, like kissing a woman." He smiled. He ran his hand over his face.

Ugh!

I shook my head. Women were nice, but I was not interested in kissing one.

He squatted in front of me and whispered, "In your case, punch someone, like, let's say me." He turned his head to the side, giving me a clear vision of his mug, and then clicked his tongue.

The desire welled up inside me, and my fist crashed into that perfect mouth.

He rolled onto his back and laughed. "Good job, only one problem, you forgot your clothes."

I glanced down to discover I was now naked. I snarled at him and snapped my fingers. My clothes reappeared along with my gear.

"Where does it go?" I asked and smoothed my leather bodice. I didn't care if he saw me naked.

That's a human problem.

The magic could have every scrap of leather in the universe as long as I had a weapon.

"Where all magic goes. Who knows?" He shrugged. His non-answer raked me wrong. My gut said he didn't know, and therefore he was giving me a bullshit answer to throw you off. He leaned against the naked statue of a lady with no arms and absently rubbed his hand over her breast.

He did it to make me uncomfortable. It didn't work. I could care less whose titty he was groping.

"We spent the first few weeks in the forest, building my strength and testing my skills. M...Pil taught me songs and trained me. Then we climbed the cliff nearby and headed east to Lanta. There wasn't much to look at and almost no humans. When we reached Lanta, the real hunt began." A smile curled my lips. The thrill of my first hunt still sang in my memories.

"You killed Govs., So what? What of the grimoire?" He urged.

"If we had it, it was in the bag. But there was nothing about the bag that would lead me to believe it was special." I reached back into the recesses of my mind, groping for the key.

"Then we must go back to the last place it was seen," he replied. He slicked his hair back and rolled his head around on his shoulders.

I took to my feet, "I have never seen it. I have no way of finding it. I don't even know where to start. You ask for the impossible!" I yelled, then added, "Master," I stopped myself before the oh-so-human words could slip out.

Begging. Yuck!

"I saw it the day you were born," he replied, sighed in irritation, and began to pace.

"I don't know where that is!" I screamed in frustration. Momma didn't speak of such things. If it didn't have to do with the hunt, it was irrelevant. She was singularly focused on her prey. Little could or would distract her.

"Ah, but I do. Come, little hunter." He thrust out his hand, and a portal formed in the middle of the room. The other side was dry flat land with a few trees in the distance along with the leftovers of a downtown cityscape.

I stepped through and came face to face with a highway sign. Most of the letters were gone. However, enough remained for me to make out the shapes of a word -- Dallas.

"This is where my father was from," I remarked.

"Yes, and Sarah too. That is not why we are here. He crossed the street and walked through the opening to a brick house. The wind picked up, and the sign rattled with the power of air. The highway couldn't be far off if the sign lay here. Yet when I looked around, the tell-tale signs of the old human highways weren't there. The scent of iron that lined those roads wasn't in the air.

There were other houses next to the one Puca entered, each covered in bricks all lacking iron.

No wonder Alice chose this place.

I stepped over the tall, dry grass and the cracked walkway to enter the house.

"Come to the back," Puca called. The floors were covered in dust piles, and the inside didn't look much different than any other abandoned house with all the windows gone. Dirt and leaves, fluffy piles for mice beds, plants that snuck in through a broken window and began growing where the dirt built up. It looked much like any other empty house from after the fall - sad, dirty, with remnants of a lost way of life.

The human part of me called to that life. To the illusion of safety, it gave off. The old-timers spoke of abundance. Anything you wanted could be had for almost nothing. This house was nothing more than the leftovers of that decadence.

The back room was different. It was clean. The door frame waked with the flavor of acorns. The color of the wakes was Momma's. She laid this spell, and it was a protection spell to keep everyone out. I glanced at Puca.

He shrugged, "There is little magic that can keep me from my heart's desire." He ran a finger over the chair rail, searching for grime. Momma liked things neat. Dirt was only a way to be tracked. He pulled his finger back clean. His eyebrows rose in surprise.

I took in the room. Bed--check, curtains for privacy -- check, there was nothing else. There was no need for another item.

"I don't see a blanket or the bag," I remarked. To be sure, I turned in place, my eyes hungry for anything Momma might have left behind. It was a fruitless search. She never made those mistakes.

Puca tapped a finger to his lips while pouting. His feet began their never-ending shuffling. He moved around the room with his dance bending with the grace of a dancer to touch a finial or examine the stitching of a rotten piece of fabric.

He finally stopped in front of me. "Call forth your tracking spell, hunter. Follow the trail."

I didn't know how to do that. I just followed the natural magic trail all creatures carried. Humans carried a watered-down version of it, but it was there.

I opened my mouth to speak and faltered. I couldn't say no. I had to find a way to track the grimoire. "Master," I gulped.

I can't fail.

The magic would eat me like a delightful treat on the end of a blade.

Puca danced around behind me and whispered into my ear, "Pil could do it. You have her blood. Do you not, changeling?"

Rage swept through me. He was questioning my status as a Fae and a hunter. Without a thought, I turned around and slammed my fist into the side of his head, "You know I do. Otherwise, why trick me into swearing my magic to you and your cause?" I growled. I changed my footing, ready for a fight. I couldn't win, but I was going to die trying.

He stumbled back and leaned into the wall, and crossed his legs. "Somewhere in your blood lays the answer to both our questions."

I rolled my eyes.

More riddles.

"What is that, prey tell?" I groaned and kicked the bed frame. I searched for the dust to shake free from the bedding. Momma didn't leave a mess. No dust fell.

"Pil, she has all the answers. We must get them from her." He pushed off the wall, jumped onto the bed, and squatted by the headboard.

"You can't receive answers from a dead Fae," I scoffed, then plopped down on the bed. The scent of acorns and grass drifted to me—it overpowered Puca's horse and leather.

Momma never smelled of grass with a hint of rain in the distance.

It dawned on me. It was me.

I smell of a far-off rain and grass... of that electric moment before the lightning strikes the ground and the thunder rolls over your senses.

I was born here and then again in the cave. I was born of Fae and humanity, forever straddling the two worlds.

"No, you can't speak to the dead. You *can* speak to the living." Puca picked a loose thread from the blanket covering the bed, and the seam fell apart.

I groaned, "Say what you mean. Enough with your riddles!"

Puca leaped off the bed, thrust out his hand, and ripped a portal into the wall. The opening only revealed the wall.

"What good is traveling to the same room." I stood up. I was done with this. I was going to return to Paris. My belly quivered at the idea. I pushed that to the side. A hunt lay there, and the magic wouldn't wait. The sensation of being pulled apart nibbled at the edges of my form. That feeling was one I didn't want to experience in full force.

I was already missing pieces of my soul from the last meal magic made of me.

Puca pulled back the portal. It snapped closed, leaving the taste of acorns heavy in the air. He pivoted and shuffled around me. I turned to keep him in my sights.

The moment I was facing the window and the bed, he reached around me and slammed a portal into the center of the room. "Now, do you see the hunt?" He whispered.

The portal opened to this very room, yet the one I saw carried Momma's magic trail along with mine.

"What is this? More Fae trickery?" I whispered. My heart grew heavy with its desire. I wanted to leap through to that world and join Momma.

"I can't leave it open. You have one Fae day to find the grimoire and return to this room. Or I will leave you in the past to relive everything. Remember that you are unable to change the past in any way," he murmured so low no one save a Fae could overhear.

My mouth dried on the implications.

Time. That is how you speak to the dead. You open a portal in time.

"Why can't I open my own portal when I have what we seek?" I replied. The scent of the open portal whispered of

Momma. My hunter's heart thirsted for my hunting companion and her love.

"Do you really want to chance it? If you open a portal in the past, I don't know what could happen. It could bring you right back here or take you to another time altogether," he stated.

My belly quivered. If I opened the wrong portal, where would it take me? If I didn't make it back, what would I do? Wander around, waiting to catch up to my own time? And Nick? What about Nick or Ron?

"Did you try?" The question withered on my tongue.

Of course, he tried.

He wanted to save her. He would have done anything to save Danu.

"You cannot change the past," he growled. Fur sprouted on his cheeks, moving down his neck at a slow pace.

"How do you know?" I demanded.

If I could go back, I could save Nick.

"Because Pil tried, many times. If she couldn't do it, it can't be done. She relived the past many times. Pil was much older than you know. She missed my portal once!" He shouted.

I whirled around, "Momma tried to save Danu?" I asked in awe. A new pride engulfed me.

"Yes," he roared, "Do you think I would be standing here if there was another way. Now, do as I demand and find the grimoire and end this evil cycle of death. One Fae day, here in this room!" He shouted and pushed me backward into the portal and onto the floor of the past.

CHAPTER 6

SARAH

Jacques didn't and wouldn't have all the pieces of the stone well without the information I alone now carried. I had moves to make.

I unlocked the room with the snap of my fingers. Whatever battle would be waged needed to happen as far from the stones as possible.

Puca said the throne once sat on the surface before Mabe gave it away to the humans.

So far, Wott and Bonn had done nothing other than sitting on their asses watching the whole show. I didn't have an oath of allegiance. They weren't my vassals. They were no better than Jacques and the rest of his ilk.

It burned me to my core. I couldn't allow them to continue to go free. They needed to join me or die. Fea could no longer be divided. I didn't care about winter courts or summer courts, Seelie, or UnSeelie. None of that mattered now. This was a battle for life and death. And if they didn't realize which side they should choose, then they needed to go. Fea needed fresh blood. Mod understood that which was why she chose the winning side.

Me.

The sycophants filtered back into the throne room. I took one disgusted look at them, curled my nose, and exited through the main door of my castle.

I snorted. It was funny. I had a castle. I was the queen of crazy, and I was about to led our entire army to fight the devil.

Hum.

My wings fluttered open, and I pushed as much air as I could underneath them as I moved toward the spring court. And Wott.

I landed just outside his castle before the moat, in the middle of the road. Right in front of me stood a pike, and on it was a leg. The blue blood had dried, running down the limb, coating the pike all the way to the ground, where soft celadon mushrooms grew. The foot still held the shoe from Finian's leg. His was similar to his brother Deston's, curled up at the end like a jester.

Part of me wanted to snicker at the stupidity of it all. The other part preened with the glory of knowing that my will was done. A pixie fluttered onto the leg, sat down, and began chewing on a piece of the rotting flesh. The exposed bone near the kneecap revealed the patella and the tendon no longer there holding it in place. Parts of the shin bone peeked through thin layers of the rotting skin. I sniffed at the scene, pulled my wings closed and close to my torso, then walked on by. The floorboards of the moat creaked with my weight.

One doesn't think of themselves as fat per se, or heavy.

I suppose I could sing for light as a feather. *Jack be nimble, and Jack be quick.*

Wings do make you heavy.

The additional bone structure necessary to carry you into the skies would bring additional mass. Or at least, one would assume that. Not that I really thought about it much.

The portico appeared to be inter-woven vines with pretty flowers. Morning Glory curled here and there with the big green leaves.

I stepped into the forecourt and watched as every Fae of the spring court froze in shock before meeting the ground crossing their fingers, covering one arm over their chest, and bowing their heads.

If I had been still human, I might have stopped to look at them. But I no longer was, so that part of me really was gone. No matter what the shade in my head said.

I strode past all of the cowering, simpering Fae, entering the castle proper to find Wott already seated upon his princely throne. He took to his feet and immediately swept down in a courtly bow.

"Don't give me your crap. I don't need to see you bow and scrape. I'm here for something completely different. You will give me your allegiance, swear a vassal tie, or you will die, and so will everyone in your court!" I announced.

Though I didn't look around, many paled. The wakes in the room smelled of uncertainty, and the walls froze with fear. Fae buildings live for their masters. Without the court to sustain them, they withered away, back to the magic.

Wott tilted his head up enough to meet my eyes.

I'd never paid much attention to the spring prince or his court.

Let's be honest. I don't give a fuck about any of the courts.

Deston's was still vacant, and Mod was doing just fine with the Swan castle.

All around were a riot of flowers and a multitude of colors dancing, one on top of the other, each vying for the attention of spring. There was a moisture in the air, hinting at the April showers that brought the May flowers. And I loved flowers.

Summer was really my choice if I had to choose a season. I liked the heat: the endless blue skies and the hot sandy beaches. I always longed for the lap of waves on my toes as I dug my feet into the sand at a beach.

But spring was nice too. Everything smelled fresh. As if the rain had just stopped and every blossom had discovered perfume. It was heavy and light, fruity-floral—a delight for the senses.

"What do I get for such a request, my Queen?" Wott asked. His eyes twinkled. He knew Janice was gone, and Jacques was free. The lust of Spring filled his manner.

He reached for my hand and pressed a kiss to the tender flesh of my palm. His eye stared me down with a deep hunger. His aura waked with sex and the promise of many pleasures.

Internally I groaned. Spring is the rutting season, the time when plants pollinate and spread their seeds. Animals vie for the right to rut and mate, creating the next generation. Everything wants to fuck.

Even the spring Prince. Why didn't I see this coming?

I didn't know.

"What do you want?" Answering a question with a question was the Fae way, and I was getting good at it.

"The power of Wyld is broken. There is no longer a curse that carries a timeless death. You are without a King, so I would offer my humble services to my Queen." His lips pulled back into a sensual smile filled with innuendo. His fingers stroked the palm of my hand as if he was my lover stroking my thigh.

I didn't need to wonder what kind of service he was offering. It was apparent in his pants. The hard-on he was sporting seemed painful, being held back by all his clothes. The pheromone-scented room sighed.

The connection between his fingers and my skin raced to my core, and I bloomed with need. My mouth hung open as his lips caressed my inner wrist. The tip of his tongue flicked at the blood vessel under the skin.

Desire rolled through me. Janice was the only one I'd ever let get this close. The only person I'd fucked. The vision of Wott between my legs performing with his tongue on my private parts filled every thought. His hands gripped my thighs to hold me in place. My nipples hardened with a needy ache.

I blinked to clear the heavy want from my eyes and body. Wott was doing something to me. It was charisma, a heady sexual power.

The wakes of lust hung in the air all around me.

My left hand illuminated, and I grabbed the wakes in the room, burning that magic away. The lust evaporated along with my patients.

What is it with the Fae? They either want to kill you or sex you up.

There was no in-between. To prove the point, the sound of moaning in the distance permeated the air. I couldn't tell if this was an orgy or a porno. Either way, I didn't want to join the Court of sex and stupidity.

I forced a sly welcoming smile over my face, then I smashed his head into the floor. "I don't need a new King," I informed him in a sticky-sweet voice. "You can keep your horny offer to yourself." I kicked him in the chest for show, which was not enough to injure, but he made a great sound with the impact. I stepped on his back and over to the throne-type chair in the room.

The seatback was too high to accommodate my wings. Rather than let a little thing like a seat backstop me from taking over, I sang the problem away.

My mom liked all kinds of music, even though she was hundreds of years old. One of the bands she liked was Tears for Fears, Songs from the Big Chair. I thought that was a funny name for an album. *Shout* was the only song that fit this situation to a 'T.'

"These are the things I could do without." The chair morphed into a low-backed chair with a cross brace in the center at the base. I took my seat. I didn't end the song there. *Oh, oh, no*, I kept going. My intent picked Wott up and placed him at my feet as a footrest.

The sick-fuck moaned as if me putting him at my feet in a submissive position was what he really wanted all along. I kicked him again, "Shut the fuck up and swear your undying servitude to me!" I shouted.

"I will, my Queen, with great glee… for a boon."

"What Boon?" I demanded. The sexy feelings started again. I internally groaned with irritation. I didn't have time for this.

"You will make me King." He stared up at me with cardinal hungry eyes.

Making him King didn't mean I'd need to fuck him. He clearly had expectations, and I wasn't playing that game. Historically there were sexless and loveless alliances/marriages. For a moment, I weighted this idea, then pushed it aside. Spring would never want that.

An Oath is a negotiation.

What would happen to Jacques if I named a new King? How did that work?

Part of me wanted to whistle for Puca. He would have the answers. Instead, I asked Wott.

"What happens to Jacques if you become King?"

"Nothing."

"Then what good is making you King? I don't need another big swinging dick with the power of a King running around." I was on my feet and the walls curled in on themselves in fear. The Spring court stopped all their cavorting and coward when faced with my anger.

"A living King cannot be stripped of his powers. Only death can do that. The magic only takes back what it's given at death or by breaking an oath." Wott's explanation hit me as hard as the magic blast that freed Jacques to begin with.

I fucked up when I made Jacques King. I was in such a hurry I didn't think there could be a blowback. Yet, the ramifications came at me from every direction. Scenarios moved through my mind as if I suddenly discovered light speed.

"No." The foot on Wott's back pushed him into the floor. "Swear or die! Fae will only survive with one leader, not 3 or 4." I pulled Silver from the scabbard on my back and placed the tip at the base of Wott's neck. The court leaned in with anticipation. The sound of feet shifting flowed around the room as various court members took a fighting stance.

"Choose," I instructed.

"Either way, it would be death. If I choose you and you lose, Jacques will kill me." His dry, mirthless laugh wasn't lost on me. Shitty choices all around are all I ever get.

"Then choose me. Bet on me. I never lose," I remarked, pushing as much charisma into my words as the magic would give me.

"My Queen."

I pushed him onto his back with my toe. He covered his chest with his left arm, crossed his fingers, tilted his head down, and touched his forehead with as much grace as the Prince to spring carried.

I stepped back to give him space to grovel and swear. Wott maneuvered to his knees and regained the Fae sign of submission. This time when he tilted his head up to gaze at me, a different male met my eyes. Gone was the playful teasing Fae filled with lust and games. This was a Fae backed into a corner with no way out. He was serious, sober, and penitent.

"Give me the oath that will buy me my life for as long as you breathe, for you are my only hope. You are also the only Fae alive to beat Jacques." A human would have slumped at this level of humbling. Wott held his head high for his court to see. He wanted to put on a good show.

I can respect that. Dignity is so important when you're leading people.

"Swear your undying loyalty to me. You will fight for me in any way I demand. You will not work against me in any way or through another. You'll keep your sex shit to yourself." I internally gagged. I was missing something, but what?

"Anyone in the Spring court not sworn to me will be put to the sword and will have their body stuck on a pike next to Finian's leg. If you fail me, may the magic rip you apart." I finished and waited. He gulped and gave me his oath. The room echoed his words, changing names and titles. The green light of a fairy oath illuminated the room to the point if someone told me the candles were now glowing green, I'd have believed them.

When most of the bowing and scraping was over, Wott stood up, took my hand, and kissed it properly without any subterfuge. "I'll call on you soon. Be ready," I opened a portal and left.

CHAPTER 7

MERCIA

For a moment, I sat there and stared at the magic trail hanging in the air above my head. Momma was close, and if I hurried, I could catch up to her.

Another scent lingered in the room. It was one of honeysuckle and soap. There was only one person I knew that smelled like that — Alice. Her cornsilk blue trail hung over a chair and exited the room alongside Momma's.

Did they leave together?

I didn't have time to worry about the company Momma was keeping because the sound of a machine screeched from a distance. The noise reminded me of my quest and the demands of magic. I was on my feet in a flash. I reached the door frame as the sound of heavy breathing reached me.

Two mouth breathers entered through the front door, cutting off my exit.

I pulled my shadowy cloak around my form and slipped back into the room. There wasn't anywhere to hide. The room held so little. The only shadows were under the bed. I moved to a corner next to the window, hoping the light shining in would blind them enough to skip over me.

The first man entered with his gun tight to his shoulder. He swept the room and moved in as his companion followed. The second one muscled the mattress off the bed frame and tossed it at me. I crouched down to allow the mattress to provide me with the cover I desperately needed.

"Well fuck, I thought for sure the pointys were in here," he huffed and lowered his gun.

"They must have just left. I mean, look how clean it is. The nark said he saw them this morning," the other man remarked and moved out to the larger room.

I held my breath and readied myself. I pulled a dagger. I closed my eyes, steadied my internal turmoil, then reopened them. The second man's steps brought him closer to the window. He stopped a foot away from me and shifted a curtain to the side. A beam of light shone into the room, illuminating the underside of my hiding place.

The man shifted on his feet and reached over, grabbing the blanket that was still covering the mattress. He pulled, and the bedding refused to budge.

I was too close to sing it free.

The man grabbed the edge of the mattress, pulling it out of the way. The beam of light from the window fell on me, and his eyes widened.

A moment later, my blade lodged itself in between his ribs while my hand covered his mouth to muffle any sound. His hand moved to the gun hanging under his arm. I changed the blade angle to the right. A gurgle erupted from his lips as blood welled up between my fingers.

His hand twitched, and the gun at his side went off, blasting a hole in the floor next to my foot. I released the man, and his body slid to the floor as I pulled my dagger free.

The other man tromped through the house, "Jon?" He yelled.

I hummed for Jacques to make me quick and leaped through the window.

There were men in the yard, stepping over old trash and broken fence posts. To my surprise, there were more houses than before. For a moment, everyone stood still in shock before their training kicked in trigger fingers took over.

Without a moment to think, I flashed to the next house, then leaped for the rotten balcony above. Light as a feather passed my lip three times before I jumped onto the gabled roof. Bullets pepper my steps, but I managed to stay ahead. I crossed over the ridge pole only to find the source of the screeching - a tank.

I tiptoed to the chimney for cover. Fire peppered both sides of the roofline.

The screeching sound came again, and I peeked out to find the main gun on the tank was maneuvering my way.

Momma called them metal demons. The sound they gave off was nothing short of a banshee on the prowl. I knew the song to destroy a tank.

The metal screeching was replaced by the deep hollow sound of metal locking into metal. The barrel rose to take aim.

I slapped both sides of my face in turn. The power of Jacques bloomed inside me.

"Humpty Dumpty sat on a wall," The rattle of gunfire in the background terminated, and all around me froze.

I moved out from behind the chimney to take in the coming carnage. My belly tightened. "Humpty Dumpty had a great fall," most of the humans in front of me fell to the ground in broken piles. Those left behind either ran for their lives screaming or cowered on the ground, covering their heads.

"All the King's horse and all the Queen's men couldn't put Fae back together again." The tank and all the houses around save the one under my feet and a few next to Momma's hidie-hole came apart, leaving only one occupant from the tank.

Major Willis.

A smile peeled across my face. I was going to enjoy this.

He stood up and screamed, "Fae," pointing his gun at me and pulling the trigger. The bullet whizzed past my head, missing, but not by much.

"I'll kill you!" He shouted. While continuing to empty his weapon and grabbing a fresh one when he ran out, he moved toward the house.

"Not before I kill you." I smiled with the knowledge that Momma would kill him in a little over a year and a half.

"You may be 3-0, but I will win in the end," he snarled.

I laughed at his bravado.

What an arrogant ass. In his world, humanity wins, and in mine, no one does.

It was funny how many sides a coin could have.

I leaped down from the roof behind the house heading away from Major Willis. I then tilted my head to the side. He couldn't tell us apart, Momma and I. Up close, our eyes would give it away. However, Major Wills never saw Momma up close.

Footsteps followed behind me. I flashed around to the front door and found Momma's acorn-colored trail. Alice's one went the opposite direction and ended in the middle of the road.

That means only one thing - Puca took her.

Momma's headed off toward a raging Fae fire in the distance.

I flashed down the street, heading in that direction. Shouts followed me along with the pounding of feet. I veered off the main street, following her, and flashed to the Fae fire. Her trail entered the flames with no exit in sight. I flashed around the edges looking for the trail to pick it up again.

On the far side, my hunter-green trail lit up next to Momma's acorn orange leading away from the burning trees.

My body moved to keep up, yet my mind pulled back. The magic wanted me to follow to get the answers I needed to fulfill my quest.

Right now, Major Willis was following me, not Momma.

If I follow her, I will lead them to her and baby me.

The magic ground down on my insides, demanding my compliance.

I can't do that to Momma or me.

The sound of machines laced the background, just barely audible over the flames.

I know where Momma is going. I can catch up to her later.

I flashed to the road close enough to the trucks to be seen, yet far enough to make a clean break. It was time to lead my prey away. The humans stared slack-mouthed at the flames.

Fae fire is entrancing.

The color alone could trick one into submission.

The heat from the Fae fire licked at my right side, warming me to my core. The remnants of mushrooms curled in on themselves as the flames cleansed the surface of their magic. The certainty that justice had been met out overwhelmed me.

I never realized what Momma was up to before I hatched. I emerged, and she gave me a hunt. That was it. Seeing the spot where she first encountered the harvesting of the dead brought on a level of rage within me I didn't know was lingering.

The Fae should never have come back to the surface after Mabe lost it to humanity. They should have stayed in their Hallowed Hills. We had no right to meddle in the working of humanity.

Jacques caused this. He caused all of this. His interference brought me here.

I pushed the rage away. The hunt took over my feelings, and I had so many feelings right now. I had to divert their attention, so I did what any good Fae would - I whistled.

They turned en-mass. Some ran toward me, unaware of the death I dealt out. Others jumped in their trucks and cranked the machines over, then turned to follow me.

I swallowed and filled my lungs with a heavy dose of hot Fae air. After that, I began to sing *'ring around the roses.'*. My voice rose over the roar of the flames, yet the notes wouldn't take. The music fell flat, and the magic never formed.

I started again, but this one, too, nothing happened. A wave of emotion moved over me, settling in my chest where it turned into the weight of a building pressing down on me. For a moment, I couldn't breathe. The humans were getting closer. I sang for Jacques to make me nimble and quick and flashed away down the road.

I stopped several hundred yards away and pulled the trigger on my crossbow, and for the first time ever, it misfired. The trigger was taut. However, no matter how many times my finger depressed it, nothing happened. I pulled the bolt from the mechanism, released the tension, and reloaded. I depressed the trigger again. Instead of a bolt flying from the end to my target, a bullet zipped past my hand, leaving a trail of blood behind.

Pixie shit!

My bow didn't work. My chest grew tighter. The sure shot missed. The pounding in my chest blocked everything else. I flashed away.

Magic doesn't make mistakes.

There had to be a reason why it wasn't working. I didn't have time to figure this conundrum out. I moved as fast as I could, hoping to outrun every Gov in the city. My body shifted mid-stride. The fur of a change moved over me. My ears perked up, suddenly more attentive to my surrounding.

The hot fiery Fae air still lingered in my chest, burning me up with questions while the magic began chewing on my insides. Not even shifting into a wolf form could change the weight of an oath or the ramifications that go with it.

CHAPTER 8

SARAH

The summer of Fae shined in my eyes. There was no reason for the light in the Hallowed Hills to be brighter here, yet it was. Before me were fields of waving grain intermixed with wildflowers, fruit, and vegetables, the likes of which the human mind could never dream because Fae stole them all.

The riot of colors painted their way across the plain, not before I settled on the arm impaled on a pike in the center of the road. It was blistered with the strength of the Fae sun. The shade was even.

Perhaps someone came and turned the appendage for a tan?

As if Finian would care at this point whether his arm carried a lopsided tan or not.

There was no castle in sight. I whirled around to find the abode of Bonn and all his summer followers, only to find nothing. From what I could tell in the spring court, the Seelie were a merry bunch. I expected the summer to be much the same, dancing under the summer sun and lazing in the warm afternoon light.

There were trees galore but not a rock structure to be had. The trees formed a forest of sorts and carried the wakes of the living. The lesson I learned in the purple forest stuck with me. At first, I rejected what my eyes were telling me and continued searching the surrounding terrain. The niggling voice in my mind wouldn't let the forest go.

An aerial view was my best choice, and I took it. With the power of my wings, I lifted for the answer I already knew was there.

The summer court lived outside in the trees like Ewoks. The main difference was the lack of hair and the pointy ears.

The forest grew closer with each step I made, revealing a dense canopy. I closed my wings and flashed to the nearest trunk.

On the forest floor stood an earth-colored Fae with umber hair and eyes. Her body was barely covered with anything at all, save a few waxy green leaves and some small white flowers. She immediately knelt, bowing her head and crossing her arms. She looked up at me with the sly smile of the young.

Without a word, she took my hand and led me to an opening in the trees where an old elm grew as a chair. For a moment, I was struck. It was a thing of such exceptional beauty.

The thought danced through my mind. If I were a regular Fae with all the choices in the world, this was the place I would want to be, under the trees running wild with the summer sun at my back. This was a place I could lose myself.

The ever-elusive smile broke over my face, pulling muscles that complained of lack of use.

"I see you feel the power of summer, and the forest calls to you." Bonn's statement broke the spell.

My smile vanished, as did my umber-tinted friend. I stood in the clearing alone.

The seat before me was vacant. Bonn chose not to sit and lord his court over me. There were no walls here to tattle and record. The summer court was hiding in the shadows of the forest.

It was just Bonn and me.

His fingers played over the twisted wood of his princely throne. "I had hoped you would come sooner. After all, anyone with eyes can see you belong here."

"Being Queen takes up all my time. Running through the forest is for the freshly hatched and lazy," I snarled even though I shouldn't have. Bonn wasn't being aggressive, and I couldn't say I was sorry.

"I've come for what's mine," I stated, leaving little doubt to my intentions.

"My oath of tie? Why didn't you come sooner? I would happily have pledged myself first. The Summer Court is your home, Sarinha, my Queen. We are all at your service." He bowed his head and crossed himself.

It wasn't a fight, and he wasn't asking for anything. It put me on guard. I didn't trust a hand offered in friendship with no caveats. Was there such a thing? There's a catch. There was always a catch.

Nothing comes for free. An oath is a very last thing on anyone's list of gimmes.

Holding my body rigid and my face as bland as possible, I asked, "What do you want in return?"

"Only that you promise to favor the summer court above all others." Bonn's ask was another path to war, a path I would never take.

I can't play favorites with the courts.

They would conspire against you for it.

"No! Choose something else," I replied.

My fingers itched to dominate him. I could use my charisma or compulsion. I could, but that was another path to an internal war.

Wott's ask was a big no. Bonn's was small, so very small. Yet it was the most poison pill of all, one I would not swallow.

"Then sing me a child. Here and now. One the color of war, sanguine and midnight. Give her the laughter of bluebells and the heart of a sponge able to absorb all the joy that the summer court can bestow on her." He opened a hand to indicate a nearby tree as a host for the child.

It was a simple request, one I should grant. However, it didn't fall in with my plans, and I didn't know how to sing a Fae into existence.

"What is to be this child's purpose?" I asked to kick the can down the road.

The summer Fae peeked out from their hiding places to observe the interplay between us. Their curiosity was stronger than their survival skills.

"Joy? Yes, I think joy will be good enough. She need do nothing other than spread joy." He tapped his lower lip in thoughtful contemplation.

"Joy sounds good. I will grant you this child." Though I didn't believe she would ever hatch. If my plans succeeded, Joy would never be. It saddened me. My heart ached for the Fae-ling that would never hatch—a lump formed in my throat.

How am I supposed to sing for Joy when all I feel is a deep abiding sadness for a child that will never make it.

Before the Queen's search and the fall, the Internet told stories of women who lost their babies. They never got over it. I didn't want to be that kind of mother to Fae. I didn't want to offer a child and take it away before it could even hatch. My insides tore at the anchors holding the organs in place.

"After Jacques is dead," I replied as even as I could muster.

Bonn began to sputter, "But my—"

"I will not create a life that may never hatch because of Jacques!" I shouted over him.

A warm hand slipped into mine and interlaced. Rather than snatch my hand away, I stared down at the Fae kneeling next to me.

Umber gazed up at me, her eyes wide with an unspoken plea.

"Burna can't speak. She hatched that way. Tatiana promised me a child. Burna was my prize. She is a quiet pleasure, tiptoeing through the forest. Summer is all about the chance to survive the winter. We are filled with nothing but promise and the optimism that comes with hope. We need something to fight for."

The entirety of the summer court stood before me, and I was shocked at how small the court was. I expected hundreds of Fae, yet there were maybe sixty. They couldn't fill a castle even if they tried.

"Where are the rest of you? The court? Where are they?" I asked and whirled around to assure myself of the numbers.

"Gone. We have not had a Queen replenish our numbers since the war of Jacques and Jillian. This is all that's left of the summer court." Bonn's statement flattened me. All the Queens were UnSeelie and unwilling to grant a boon to a Seelie prince. They only saw them as adversaries.

When Puca spoke of an imbalance, I didn't realize how far it reached. Even the courts were off. The spring court was filled to capacity with all manner of Fae while summer dwindled away.

It didn't matter that I didn't know what song to sing to form a Fae child. Summer needed them more than anything. A summer without love and hope was nothing more than winter with sun.

The cold only lives in your heart and not on your skin.

Fae had flocked to the powerful UnSeelie for too long.

"Swear to me, and I will give you a hundred children."

Every summer Fae fell to their knees and spoke as one of their undying fealty and an oath to save Fae no matter the personal cost. Their undying fealty humbled me. To them, I was their last and only hope.

The only voice that didn't join the rest was Burna's. She mouthed the words, and though no sound came out, the magic wrapped around her, sealing her vow. She hummed, and a wreath of flowers appeared on my head to hide the thorny crown. The scent of daises and hyacinth floated over me.

"I can fix your voice."

Burna shook her head, then mouthed, "Save your strength for the young and the war. Don't waste it on me."

"We need Fae with pure hearts as much as anything else." I cupped her cheek, then moved my hand to her throat. The magic wakes spoke of intention. The Queen who made her left out a connection necessary to work the voice box in her throat. She gave the gift of life and took away her ability to grow with magic. Burna was youthful because she couldn't grow beyond that. The magic she could wield was simple. More so than even my mother's. Even an Alice song was out of reach for Burna.

Most of the healing I'd performed was to repair. This was a full rebuild, and I wasn't sure I was up to the challenge.

Who am I kidding? Of *course, I'm up to it. I can't back down.*

I sang an old swing song by the Big Bad Voodoo Daddy's, *Hey, Lou, I want to be like you.*

The summer Fae circled us, humming along with my song, each singing with me at the chorus. Burna's mouth opened for a silent scream. Her body glossed with sweat as her face contorted in pain.

The magic curled around us. We were all part of the spell. Our song grew to not only heal her but give her the magic she was denied at creation.

When the song ended, Burna lay on her side, sobbing. Her summer brothers and sisters took turns comforting her.

"What was that?" I asked Bonn.

"Empathy is all you need to heal. Most Fae don't have it and, therefore, can only heal those they love. In the summer court, all are empaths. Yet, we can't heal what never was. Only a Queen can add in something new." His broad kind smile was a balm.

My heart was aching and emptied from all the Fae bullshit. This was the only place I felt at home in all the Hallowed Hills. "How long does a Fae take to reach maturity and hatch?" We didn't have time to wait months for a new group of the summer court.

"Danu could grow a Fae in a day," he remarked, then looked around at what I could only assume were his advisers. "All other Queens took weeks to hatch."

"Jacques can't have a Fae day, let alone weeks. That would be years on the surface. Janice and Nick don't have that long. Jacques' army of blood Fae would be enormous and well trained. No, we can't wait that long." I began to pace.

There was another way. I knew there was. I just had to figure it out.

Blood. Blood is the only way.

We needed blood, and a lot of it. "All of you come with me." I lifted my wings into the Fae light and jetted for Deston's principality and what was left of his court.

CHAPTER 9

MERCIA

I made it to the edge of the rubble-laden city, near a river. The water was clear and moved at a lazy pace, unaware of the turmoil all around. Trees spotted the landscape here and there, creating pockets of tranquil shadows. One tree hung over the water at an odd angle as if pushed over by a strong hand. The underside was part of the riverbank, dark and cool.

I shifted back to my Fae form and joined that cool air while pulling my hunter's cloak tight to hide. The sound of humans in the distance reached me.

Were they coming this way? Should I cross the water and find a new shadowy blind or wait to see if they pass?

Fear is a virus. Once introduced into the body, it replicates if not held in check. I'd tasted fear too many times in the last year, and I'd grown used to the flavor. It came too easy and no longer tasted foreign.

Staying here in my hiding spot was precipitated by fear — my fear of dying, my fear for Momma and baby me. I spit the taste of that fear onto the ground as if venom sucked from a snake bite. If the only way to rid myself of that crippling fear was to suck it out, I would cut my body to ribbons and bleed myself dry.

Then it struck me.

What did Puca say? "You can't change the past."

Baby me wouldn't die here and now. I couldn't. Otherwise, I couldn't be here now as a full-grown Fae.

I wanted to smack myself in the head.

But how had I destroyed all those houses and men with my song? Well, not all of them.

Unless I was always going to kill them.

Major Willis didn't die. But I knew he wouldn't because Momma killed him later.

If I couldn't change the past, then neither could they change the future.

Does that mean I can't die here?

I puzzled over this for some time. Yet, like the stones of Danu, it too was a circle that only gave me a headache. I wasn't going to figure it out.

Traveling in time is a science fiction novel, one that people read to forget about the real world. I needed to live in the real world, not fantasy.

The humans picked the area over for some time, but they scurried away to hide as the sun went down. In the human mind, the Fae still ruled the night here. The fall was not as far off at that time. The complacency of my time hadn't settled over mankind.

When the last of the sun's rays disappeared over the horizon of this flat land, I emerged with my hunter cloak intact. I flashed back to the outskirts of Dallas to pick up Momma's trail. It led me to a large stucco building surrounded by cattle bones. Thousands of cows died here. Most of the exterior of the building had lost its smooth finish. The apex of the front lay on the ground next to a large bronze bell.

I ran my hand over the patinaed object. At one time, it gave a pure sound for all-around to hear. I respected anything that could sing with clarity.

Other than the resting place of the bell, there was nothing here. I couldn't imagine what Momma was doing here. There was nothing of value and no food.

I stalked my way around the area and came across a Fort Worth Stockyards sign. That explained the graveyard of cow bones. The tinkle of water came from up the road, and I made my way there.

It was a watering hole for livestock and horses. A few animals scurried away at my approach. I'd interrupted their late-night drinking. The creatures were nothing more than vermin, yet the black stripes and ringed eyes brought a smile to my face. I asked them whether they'd seen a Fae pass their way.

All stared at me with wide eyes and shook their heads in fear.

These creatures weren't like the flittermice. To them, I was a predator. Flittermice saw us as equal partners in the hunt. Our prey was very different, making us allies and not rivals.

The raccoons raced away as soon as my back turned, and I didn't bother to give chase.

Momma's trail went north, then west. Finally, she turned east. I believed she was going to finally head for the cave and sing me into my chrysalis, only for her trail to loop back down before heading north again.

I lost her several times and had to backtrack. My only clue to follow at one point was the dead bodies along her trail. I vacillated over heading to the cave and waiting for her or continuing the hunt.

The hunt won.

The next town was inhabited by humans. None carried the Fae shine all-around a town square. There was a well for water and big trees. The people had rigged a pump from the well to the local fields for irrigation. I smiled to myself. My old CB had hydroponic grow rooms. The food wasn't great, but it was edible, and in the world, after the fall, you couldn't ask for more.

For a lark, I sang. No sooner had the music drifted from my lips than the ground changed, and the plants perked up. The magic took, and I heaved a sigh of relief.

The magic worked. Perhaps the sure-shot and the song were a fluke.

Did the Fae fire suck all the magic away?

I slunk around the edge of town, working my way to the other side and Momma's trail. I found the trail, but I found something else—a dead body.

The chest was slashed open near the heart. The skin was shrunken and sallow. The eyes hollowed out and emptied as if the fluid in them leaked away.

The bloody handprint on the chest told me why he died.

Me. Momma killed him to fuel me. To keep me alive.

I laid two fingers on his neck, checking for a heartbeat I knew wasn't there. This was the cost of my existence. This man's death.

His skin was lukewarm.

He died not long ago.

I took to my feet, chasing Momma's trail as fast as my magic would take me. I flashed along the dry plains, hoping to catch up. I came to a red river. The color was apparent even in the deep darkness.

Momma's trail ran cold. It ended at the river's edge. There was no double back or skip along. Just the end. As if Puca had plucked her from the river's edge and whisked her away.

I counted out the days in my head. Twenty-five, twenty-five days, and I had nothing to show for my troubles.

One Fae day was the equivalent of several months. Maybe six? This month was almost gone, and I was no closer to catching up than the day I arrived.

I could scream and throw a fit.

I can find a pet to enlist to my cause if the magic would let me.

I sang '*Come back, Peter, come back, Paul,*' asking the magic to bring me a floating log in the river. But it fell flat, leaving me with no choice but to head for Louisiana and the cave.

It was the only sure thing.

At this rate, I would miss the portal, and then what? Watch the world go by, unable to defend myself unless the magic deems it so?

No Fucking Way!

*****

I stuck to the top side of the cliff, behind the cave, well away from Momma's hunting ground. The magic didn't stop me from watching her.

My memories of Pil were of a giant Fae with the power to destroy the world if they got in her way. The creature I spied on for my every waking moment was not the same person. She didn't stand so tall. Her eyes searched for the hunt in a tired, sad fashion way. The zest I tasted when we were on the prowl wasn't there. She was hollow.

She sang only for the simple things and barely that.

It tore at me. I wanted to race down there and tell her I lived. But that would be changing the past, and the magic wouldn't let me do that. Every time I made a move to speak to her, an invisible wall stopped me until I moved back.

Time was flying by, and I only had four days left to get what we needed. The magic demanded I do my job and kept me from full filling my quest at the same time.

I screamed, yet no sound came from my lips. Every song I sang never fruited into magic. I was trapped in this in-between world, being tortured. The magic ate away at my insides a little more with every second that slipped by.

I called to a flittermouse, hoping beyond hope they would hear me and bring me the answers I needed.

One turned on his wing and glided down to my shoulder, and landed with the grace of youth. He offered me a greeting and asked why I hid in the trees instead of joining my sister Fae in the cave.

I didn't know how to answer the question.

"The magic won't let me," I replied, hoping he could understand.

He chirped in agreement, then informed me — many times, he attempted to inform Pil of my presence only to find his mouth held shut.

Interesting.

He asked my name, and I gave it to him. He chirped a greeting and said he wouldn't forget. As he winged away, I found a small brown mark on his belly. This flittermouse was the old-timer from the battle for New Orleans.

I sang for health and wealth for all his days. The magic took hold, wrapping around the small leathery body and glowing with a power only magic carries.

He lived that long because of me. I did it to him. It was meant to be. It made me smile to know that I had given my old friend such a long life. He deserved it more than most.

*****

Four days. That is all there was left. It would take me three to reach Dallas and the town of Garland, where I was born. I had one day left to make this happen.

I left the area and stood on the old dock, looking out over the marshland. Then it came to me. I needed to get Momma to sing the song. I didn't need to be *here*. I could find the grimoire on my own. I just needed the song.

That was easy to do. I knew about when she sang it and sort of where. I just needed a ride.

And if I don't leave now, I will miss this one.

Momma popped out of the cave in the distance. Twilight was fresh on the wind, and the trees provided additional darkness to hide her from the evil sun. She stretched, then called for our nighttime friends.

There was so much I wanted to know and say. I wanted just to stand by her side for a moment and breathe an easy breath of the forest air. The pain of missing Momma came to me fresh and sharp. The magic pulled at my insides, reminding me of my obligations and the need for both Fae and humanity. I blew a kiss on the breeze and headed away.

I flashed to the long-forgotten border of a country that didn't exist and kept going. I stayed within the trees as much as possible and away from water where humans were sure to be.

Texas is a big place when all you have are your two feet to carry you around. I wanted to bleed a round and take to the air. But the terrain was too flat. I would be an easy target in such a landscape.

I kept going when the sun finally set on the second day. I sang for sixpence to keep going. Only the magic had other ideas, so the tune was stifled and tinny.

My frustrated screams filled the dry air. I slapped both cheeks, hoping for the rush that normally came. It, too, was just out of reach. My belly clenched down the problem. I paced around the tree and tried again.

Maybe if I move locations, the magic will take over here.

That didn't work either. There was nothing for it. I was too tired to flash another inch, and the magic wouldn't give me a boost. So I pulled my hunter's cloak over my body and laid down to sleep.

I awoke to the sound of a horse in the distance. I rolled over and took in the position of the sun. It was too high in the sky to be morning. My feet found the ground, and I moved at the speed of the wind. I spied the horse, which was having a snack in the shade.

Flashing wasn't meant to be done for hours on end. I did it anyway. Rather than trying to avoid humanity, I made a beeline to Garland. I didn't have a moment to waste.

My feet hurt, and I flashed again. The sun set quickly that day. I kept going through the night, grinding my teeth at the waste of time this entire trip was.

How many times did Puca make Momma do this before he gave up? Ten, twenty? A hundred? The magic cut into my chest with its need. I gasped at the pain of it.

Even in New Orleans, it wasn't like this. This wasn't a nibble around the edges. It was a bite. A large carnivorous mouth full. The magic tore it away from my soul, and the feeling of missing a piece of oneself was no different from the piece of my heart Nick carried with him.

I was quickly disappearing, and there was little I could do to end it.

The sign marking this area as Dallas loomed in the distance. My feet found a new gear, and I sped up. The door to Momma's house opened into the darkness beyond. Only shadows lingered in there. The area was devoid of noise or magic.

I flashed past the lintel and into the bedroom in time to watch the portal snap closed as my finger touched the remaining wake. The magic ripped a little more of me away.

The tip of my finger bloomed with blood. It was the only piece of me to make it into the portal.

A roar welled up from deep within and shook the house. I moved to destroy the room, only to have the magic hold me in place. I couldn't take my anger out on anything.

"What's the spell?" I screamed. The sound waked away, leaving me a lump on the floor.

My need to rain fired down on the world, and the magic released me. My eyes ached for sleep, and my mind cried.

"Why can't I get a break?" I shouted.

"Because you and your kind are an abomination," the deep voice from the other room replied.

I whipped around with my crossbow at the ready, only to find the black barrel of a gun waking with the iron bullets it carried.

Major Willis' face broke into a wide smile. "I knew you'd be back." He patted himself on the back. I stared him and the problem down. I couldn't shoot him.

The bow won't work. The magic will stop it.

I couldn't sing for the same reason.

"Why don't you come along quietly, and we will get you a nice room to sleep in while we run some tests." He held his other hand out in invitation.

Does he think I was weak and unable to fight back?

I took in the scene. I sang, yet nothing happened. My finger was bleeding, and the magic stopped me from moving.

I glanced from his gun to his hand and his face. It dawned on me - he had two hands.

The magic won't stop this one.

The dagger was out of its sheath, slicing his hand off before he could blink. Blood spurted from the stump. A withering howl filled the room, followed by the report of a gun. The walls waked back the noise. Momma left nothing to chance. The magic protecting this room was a sound barrier—everything in, nothing out.

I smiled down at my prey. When Momma killed him, he only had one hand. She was angry because someone had cut away part of her quarry. She felt that revenge belonged to her alone. I pushed his head back so his screams could fill in the empty spaces in the room and my ears. It was heaven—my first taste of it in months.

I'd gotten my pound of flesh, and there was nothing Momma could do about it.

The sigh of a flower's death informed me there were more Govs in the surrounding area. They didn't think about where they stepped and the flowers tattled on them. There was a cry with every death in nature. You just had to know how to listen.

I had no way out and no guarantee the magic would allow me to defend myself.

I hummed a protection bubble over the house and did what every Fae in history has ever done when in need - I whistled for my one-time King and Master -Puca.

The bars of music had barely left my lips when the wall near the screaming Major shivered and split to reveal a portal, allowing Puca to step through.

He looked down at the screaming man, opened a new portal, and shoved Major Willis through. I winked at the Major just before the magic slammed closed.

"Now, pray tell, who are you and what do you want," Puca asked while slicking his hair back. He was naked from the waist up as usual. Normally, I would have soured on his attire or lack thereof. Not this time, nope. I was downright giddy to see my master and finally have the upper hand. He didn't know who I was.

For a moment, the full truth of the situation tasted sweet. Puca was at a loss. A smirk pulled at my face until a smile replaced it.

"Reopen the portal," I stated.

He scoffed, "What do I get if I do?"

The wall next to me split, and the magic blasted into the space.

Puca's mouth fell open.

My nostrils flared with delight, "Nothing," I laughed and leaped through the opening.

CHAPTER 10

SARAH

The walls of Deston's castle were gone, and only the towers holding up the arched portico were left. In the road, before the moat bridge, was a pike with a leg speared on it. I wanted to chuck it in the moat and let the flesh-eaters residing there have a meal. But that didn't send the message I needed the winter court to receive.

I'd only come back here the one time since I became Queen. Now due to the knowledge I had, I saw the castle with very different eyes. I was too scared before to notice the little touches denoting winter. The holly that lined the stone worked as anchors, holding the stone together.

Edelweiss grew all around the castle's base, edging the moat as a hedge. The trees were pines similar to the forest near the Rhine in Germany. Dead bows from the trees lay everywhere—the rust-colored needles lay in piles with branches here and there, while mistletoe hung limp and dead from the bottom of the portico.

Even the air was colder than I remembered.

Fae peeked out from behind stone and debris, curious at why their Queen had arrived.

I flew over the moat bridge and landed in the courtyard. The main doors to the castle were caved in, and the wall blocking the throne room from the outside was nothing more than rubble on the ground. Deston's pussy-willow covered throne sat undisturbed on the dais waiting for me. I whistled at the walls to reinforce them and took my rightful seat.

The winter court came out in force. Most didn't bow. Some even sneered in disgust. I stared through the lot of them, letting the disrespect slide over me.

What I am about to do will put an end to all of this.

If my plan worked, the petty divides of the court wouldn't matter in the end.

The summer Fae moved behind me in the enormous room, showing not only their support but guarding my back. I breathed a sigh of relief. For the first time since I'd entered the Hallowed Hills, I didn't feel alone. The summer court was my brethren, and the feeling of family was good. The tight vice in my chest was still there, but I didn't feel like I had to carry it all by myself.

A female moved before me. Her clothes lacked the previous charm of before when she tortured Olive. Now, she held her head high with pride. I wanted to knock her down a mark or two.

She doesn't see me for the threat I am.

Her white hair hung down her back in great braided ropes. Intertwined in the braids were baby breath and holly.

She waked with purpose.

The female crossed her left arm over her chest, "My Queen—"

"Stop!" I raised my hand and pushed her to the floor. "I only want to hear one thing." I raised my voice for all of the winter court to hear. "An Oath of Allegiance."

The Fae in front of me paled.

"My Queen," Bonn whispered, "Perhaps if we gather the court together, this will move along at speed?"

My left index finger waved him away.

I sang a nursery rhyme: *"Cold and raw the north wind doth blow, Bleak in the morning early, All the hills are covered with snow, And winters now come early."*

The Fae of the court began to trickle in. Their white coloring resembled the bleak gray of a cold winter night, each snowflake unique in style and design. The rhyme drew them home to the seat of power in the winter court. As they entered the courtyard and then the throne room, the temperature began to rise. There were thousands of Fae in the winter court.

Summer had almost none, while winter flourished with followers.

Jacques' betrayal of Danu ensured something like this would happen. His lack of foresight created this problem. Everywhere I looked was more proof of Jacques' interference and the ramifications.

"Swear your allegiance to me and Fae or join your former Prince," I stated.

Many knelt and swore without another thought. Their hair rapidly changed color to black, and they joined the summer court. These were the simple Fae. Not the ones I needed to begin with.

I needed old Fae, the ones who had seen the war of the Queens, and chose Jillian.

My wings flared and pulled me to my feet. My quicksilver sword was in my hand at the ready. Some of the winter courts began to run. The summer Fae blocked the exits and brought many to kneel before me.

I sang a shield over the castle to keep my prey in. It was a hunt of sorts. It was too easy. The walls whispered and shook. They didn't like the turn of events. They were enjoying the Wyld of winter court. The room grew cold. The walls favored me before I took the throne. They fed me and provided protection.

Janice's words came back as a blow to my solar plexus. *These walls were sworn to Deston and the UnSeelie for thousands of years. They may like you, but they will never side with you.*

"The reign of Wyld will never be over as long as Jacques lives. He killed your Prince to free himself and used Finian to do it. He turned a member of your own court against its Prince. His brother and twin." Some of the faces were swayed. They gazed at the ground in fear and sadness, an emotion most Fae never encountered. I had to crank up the fear factor.

Fae would fight to save themselves over everything else every time. "If that isn't reason enough to side with me against Jacques, then this information should be. Jacques is using Fae blood to turn humans into magic users. To make them like us. When he has a large enough army, he's going to come down here and kill every last pure Fae alive to feed his army. He will seat a new Queen, and through her, he will rule this world forever."

There were gasps.

Good!

"There are no Fae left on the surface — only changelings. Why should we care what happens to them?" A male I recognized from my days at Deston's court shouted. His midnight blue eyes probably matched his blood.

"Because magic changes you. Every time you use it. Those changelings carry the ability to become full-blooded Fae. With every song they sing, they grow stronger."

"It would take a lifetime for a changeling to even come close to a full-blooded Fae," he snarled in return. Some from his group sneered in agreement.

"So, we should look the other way while Jacques kills children?" I asked. Many shifted on their feet, not willing to speak their thoughts. "You must choose a side. This is a war. I lived as a human once. Whatever humanity I had is gone, burned away by the stone throne. I'm clever, yet there are humans ten times as cunning. If they have magic… They will use more than a song to fight, and they will win if we don't band together." I shook my head. I didn't want to seem scared, but I was.

No one invents methods to kill quite like humanity.

I wanted every last Fae to understand what we were facing. Jacques was mad, madder than a hatter, in every way.

"He doesn't want you. He won't protect you. He's given up on Fae. You are nothing more than a DNA treatment for his new army. He will cut you apart, take out your magic and inject it into a human."

A murmur started in the room. Green flashes colored the walls as winter Fae swore here and there to stop him and help me in any way. Many of the oaths were only for this war.

Once Jacques is dead, this alliance is over.

It was good enough for me. I didn't want to kill them all.

I sang for the shield to release all who were my vassal. Many left to join Mod and her court. I was left with a hundred or so winter Fae, each defiant and ready for a fight.

I whistled them into a line, "This is your last chance." I waited for a moment.

A female fell to her knees, "I cannot swear to you. I gave myself to Jacques ages ago. I can't take the magic back. I would, but I can't." She didn't beg. Her eyes spoke of sorrow and regret.

I turned to Bonn, "Take her to an iron room and lock her up. We can't risk her giving us away." He grabbed her and sang to shut her mouth and drug her away.

I began slashing. The first Fae fell to the stone floor. The gash from her chest pumped her lifeblood away and a giant mushroom formed on the floor. I thrust my hand into her chest and sang *Rock, a bye baby*.

The music rolled off my tongue and filled the room. The blood from the Fae flowed from my hand to my song, and the mushroom before me formed several chrysalides, each the colors of summer. They grew to epic proportions. An inner light illuminated the shapes inside, and in moments they began to move. Within minutes, one hay-colored chrysalis hatched, and a new Fae fell to the floor on her feet.

Parts of her husk clung to her hair and torso. She lifted her head, "My Queen. I'm Joy," she stated and smiled.

I choked on a cry. She was beautiful in her bright hay coloring. Her eyes were of dark honey that flashed gold in the light. Her hair was black as volcanic soil. She sang her husk down from the mushroom and fashioned a skirt to cover her privates, then she brushed the hair of the Fae I killed back from her face.

"She gave her life for me?" She asked, her voice filled with deep abiding sorrow.

The Fae's body was shrunken and devoid of color. You could hardly see that she once was a beautiful gray of winter.

The other Chrysalis hatched, and their Fae called me *mother* or *Queen* in turn.

My right hand was covered in blood, and my left one was lit with the power of fire. I gazed down the line of winter Fae, calculating how many new Fae would come from each one.

I promised summer hundreds, but I could give them thousands. That wouldn't be right. It would only continue the imbalance. I moved to the next holdout and killed without mercy.

Winter is cold and makes no distinction between the innocent and the guilty. Neither will I.

By the time I was finished, the court was filled with new Fae for summer and what was left of winter.

Only now, the numbers were about even.

CHAPTER 11

MERCIA

My feet stumbled as I changed from the past to the present. Time travel is a soup you swim through to reach your goal. I didn't want to swim in another bowl. Stepping into the past was a lesson in frustration and patience, one I didn't want to repeat but was going to anyway.

"You have succeeded?" My master inquired.

I looked down on my momentary defeat and shook my head, then gazed up into his hard canary eyes, "I have a plan."

"Does this plan include success?" He demanded. His features shifted from Fae to canine, though the change never took hold.

"Yes. I need you to send me back to where Momma sang her spell to find the stones. I can't interact with her. The magic won't let me. But I can watch and listen, and that is all I need to do." It was a sound plan, one with a high degree of success. As far as I knew, no one else was there.

The magic will keep me from fucking it up.

He twirled in place, his black hair spinning with him. He kickball-changed once to the left, then right, and pivoted to stand behind me.

"I don't know what day exactly she found the well cave. You will need to stay hidden, and there is nowhere to hide." He remarked. His scent of leather and horse surprise me. I didn't see him as the tranquil grass-eating horse. He rarely ever took that form for me. To me, Puca was a predator, a wolf on the prowl, ready for the fight and the kill.

I wanted to rest. Instead, I slapped my cheeks and sang for sixpence and waited for my master to open a new portal.

Puca stepped around me, inspecting my form. "You are thin. Parts of you seem barely there," he remarked. He ran a finger down my cheek. "You smell, and that smell will only grow with the blood covering your face and clothes."

I grunted in response. My personal toilet was none of his business. A smell on a hunt can make all the difference between a kill or be killed, and I had no double Momma would kill me if she caught me.

Puca snapped his fingers, and the grime vanished along with the coppery scent of human blood. A scent that would be out of place in the Hallowed Hills as much as a gun.

The portal opened to reveal a rock wall and the sound of falling water. My feet were eager to meet the past, and I moved to step through.

"Wait!"

I froze mid-step.

"The cave on the bottom, two to the left from the cave Pil takes, will lead you directly to the well chamber. It is cloaked with a glamor from the other side. It will allow you to get what you need," he stated.

My eyes wandered to meet his for a moment. He nodded his head, urging me on along with the magic and my oath.

The cave system I stepped into was more of an echo chamber than tunnels to the well. Every sound I made created fifty more of the same and carried this way and that. My movement ceased while I listened to the space.

Behind me, the sound of a knife scraping along rock came from a distance. I turned at the noise to find Momma making her way toward me in the tunnel behind the water.

My first instinct was to hide. That would only peak Momma's hunting desires. Instead, I chose to mimic her. If she believed I was her reflection, she would ignore me, and at the last moment, I could hide. She shadow danced with me for a few minutes, and I followed along as best I could.

Suddenly a laugh filled the echoing space.

Momma's laugh.

It was filled with joy. It was a type of laugh I didn't know Momma could make. The laugh I knew was filled with rue and vinegar.

She reached the falling water, and I slipped into the necessary cave and made my way to the well cave. Momma's voice sang to find her way, and she yelped once before being deposited in the well cave.

I wanted to snicker, yet before I could get a sound out, the magic choked it back, silencing me. It was a harsh reminder that I was only a spectator here with no ability to change anything.

Momma wandered around the sphere-shaped cave before stopping next to a golden flower. A similar bloom resided in Sarinha's throne room. Only hers was black and white. This was as pure a gold as I'd ever seen in or out of the Hallowed Hills. It vibrated with a power I'd seen before somewhere.

Momma stared at it for some time before going back to her task. Aqualis arrived to mock Momma and her quest to the surface. The Elements were no friends to Fae. They lingered like a fog, obscuring everything but providing no illumination.

This time was no different. Aqualis refused to help Momma.

What if she had? Would my dad have lived?

I wondered about that for a while until Momma went up through the hole in the ceiling. It was some time before Momma returned, and the sound of stone on stone reached me along with her screams of frustration.

The rock around me shook. The air changed. At first, it was just a hint of something in the air, then a taste, before the puffs created when I breathed disappeared.

I stared into the cave where Momma was singing a tracking spell that didn't take before she took out a red stone.

All the blood from my head drained into my shoes. The stone waked with her heartbeat, and she sang again.

"My Jack in the box springs up, up, up."

The stone rose,

"My Jack in the box goes round, round, round."

Like a top on its tip, the rock spin in the air.

"My Jack in the box falls down, down, down.

Help me, Jack."

The song ricocheted off the rounded walls in every direction, bouncing again and again. The stone flashed red, blinding me. A moment later, the glowing outline of the stone well began dropping down the well hole in the ceiling.

It was time to leave, and I turned away from the scene and dashed to the main cavern. The tunnel grew warmer with every step. At the main junction, I stopped.

This is where Puca will open the portal.

The sound of Momma's leather soles slapping the stone followed me, echoing around the main cavern.

I search for a proper hiding place. There were only the yawning openings to more tunnels, none providing a stitch of protection. I pulled my hunter's cloak and leaped to the tunnel with water falling to hide the exit. I hunched down and waited for Momma to pass and the portal to open.

The glowing outline of the stones floated out with Momma hot on its trail. She never even sensed me. I didn't know if I should be proud or sad.

The wall of the cavern opposite me began to steam—the water on the ground boiled with heat while the walls glowed with the swirling Fae designs, each a curling snake, twisting back on itself and out again.

The water at my feet too warmed with the surrounding rocks.

Soon, I will not be able to stay in this place.

I sang for *light as a feather* to keep my feet cool. I reached out to steady myself and looked down at the floor of the cavern. The wall burned the tips of my fingers and the meat of my palm. I snatched my hand back and shook the heat away.

"Puca, you better get on with it. I'm not whistling again!" I shouted. The skin on my palm itched with pain, and I thrust into the warm water at my feet. It did little to pull the heat away from my skin.

The rocks in the room rumbled and crashed. Chunks pulled from the molten walls before they smashed together to form Ignis.

"You are here for the stones too?" She asked. The hot stone was a lacework over her body, creating delicate patterns only fire can imagine.

"No, I am here for a song," I replied, wishing I had a mushroom round to pull my body from the waking heat that was beating at me.

"Pil has left. Why do you not go?" She walked over the hot lava-covered floor as if it was no more than a cold stone path.

My mouth opened to reply. However, no sound came out. I snapped my jaw shut to hide my problem.

No need for an elemental to learn my business.

If the magic didn't want me to share, who was I to argue?

Not that I can.

She looked me over with keen blazing eyes. "You are not right. The minerals that make you speak of another time and place. You should not be here," she growled. Her eyes flared with the inner fire of an elemental.

My belly quivered. I knew of no way to fight an Elemental.

Her body blended into the rock on the floor and flowed up the wall to join me in my tunnel.

I sang for a protection spell that didn't take. "Fuck!" I screamed.

She coiled back and raised an arm to swing, and I had no way to stop her. The magic locked me up. "I will send you back to the magic. Fae have mettled enough in the natural order." She released her power, and I watched in horror as her molten fist grew to be ten times the size.

The cavern blasted with the power of a portal, ripping the magic in half. I ducked under her blow and dove off the tunnel ledge, through the portal, and onto the floor of Momma's house.

I laid on my side for a moment, heaving in the cool air and breathing out the intense heat. I pushed the sweat back from my brow and laughed.

"I thought I'd have to whistle for you twice," I remarked, coughing.

"It wouldn't have worked," Puca replied dryly.

I rolled onto my back. "Why not?"

"Because I don't remember you doing it." He stated and crossed his arms. He was irritated.

Why should I care? He wasn't about to be boiled alive and pummeled to death by fire.

"Ignis was there," I stated, then sat up to wipe my face on my sleeve.

"That explains a few things. Did you get the song?" Puca demanded.

I nodded. He handed me a water sack. I took a big gulp, then poured some of it over my head. The cool water ran in rivulets down my hair and shoulders. I didn't care. I was still burning up inside.

"Well, what are you waiting for?" he shouted, shuffling around the room.

"What is the blanket made of?" I asked.

I took to my feet, ready for the answer I knew was coming and what I must do.

"The blood and bone of the keepers. Each witch poured a piece of herself into the quilt. Even Alice," he explained.

"Blood?" I asked. I needed to be sure. "Your witches, from your line?"

He shivered and waved his hand for me to get on with it.

"Blood calls to blood," I stated, then palmed my finger dagger. This had to be quick.

Puca turned away from me to pivot in his normal dance. I slashed his back open to the bone.

The initial scent of fresh Fae blood isn't copper like a human. It's sweet like sugar that's been cooked too long. His blue blood flowed down his body to land on the ground in a sugary, sticky mess.

I would only get one chance at this, so I sang for my life.

"My Jack in the box springs up, up, up."

Puca slipped to the ground while some of his blood floated up,

"My Jack in the box goes round, round, round."

The bloody glob swirled into a small funnel-shaped tornado.

"My Jack in the box falls down, down, down. Help me, Jack."

The blood jetted out the window, and I flashed to follow.

Puca roared with laughter. I couldn't look back. My fear-flavored virus kept me focused on the blood and my task.

CHAPTER 12

SARAH

I returned to my castle with most of the courts in tow. The Fomorians flanked me, yet I hardly noticed them. Their leader came within earshot, "Come."

"Yes, Queen," he replied.

"Gather your forces! We are going to the surface. Bring whatever you need for a fight." They weren't expendable, but every fighter mattered at this point.

I didn't want to face the truth. Janice is probably gone, and Nick too. Jacques used them to grow his army, and I was fighting for what was left of the bodies.

My wing gave out for a moment at the thought, and I stumbled as I hit the ground. My eyes burned with the unshed tears, and my chest grew tight. The shelf of bottles I kept locked away inside me rattled as I shoved these emotions into a new one and placed it along with the others marked *don't drink.*

At some point, I'm not going to be able to bottle my feelings up anymore.

I barely noticed my footsteps through the forecourt into the throne room. Lavender entered from the back door and met me at the throne.

"There's no word from Puca or Mercia," she stated, keeping her voice low. Her coloring had faded. It was no longer the bright lavender of her name. She was the washed-out lilac just before it rots and falls into the dirt. This was wearing on all of us.

If my plan worked, Lavender could forget about all of this. She would never need to give it another thought. She could weave her creations to her heart's delight.

"It doesn't matter. We're leaving." I stared into the cavernous room, my face blank of all emotion. "One last thing. When," I didn't want to say *if*, "Mercia and Puca return if they need the library, let them in." I hummed to change the shield keeping everyone out. It was a risk, yet, if they were to come through with the blanky, they might need a safe place to inspect it.

Lavender stepped back, giving me the space I needed.

"It is time," I announced, "We can't wait another Fae day. Jacques gains more human witches with every second we waste here. I lift the ban on visiting the surface. Every Fae, find a round or bleed one! We leave in twenty beats of a pixie's heart." The court echoed with my proclamation. The walls shivered, and all the flowers turned to nuts. Even the walls wanted to protect the seeds for the future.

My hands began checking knives and daggers. Silver lay nestled in my scabbard, pulling down on my waist. The weight was reassuring. For once, I had good shoes, and a small smile cracked my face. My boots were different from the pair Arty and I stole from the mall. Those were long gone. It felt like a lifetime since I'd driven Pastor Rollin's jeep and run from the gangs on the surface. That life was more of a movie that I watched once and like to think about. This me began the day I chose to come back to the Hallowed Hills and not stop until this battle was over. All the Fae faces that stared back at me were part of my new life.

Bonn tilted his head to me, while Wott threw me a wink and a kiss. The winter court clumped together leaderless. Their chins were raised in defiance against any Fae that questioned their loyalty.

I threw them a nod of acknowledgment.

The autumn court gathered behind what I could only assume was Mod's seneschal. A male Fae with nut-brown color marking and eyes. He crossed his arm over his chest and nodded to me while mouthing, "My Queen."

The throne grew cold for me. Whatever happened on the surface, I didn't think I was going to sit on that rock again.

Moving to the forecourt and then out into the fields surrounding my castle, I waited for my army to follow me. The Fomorians clustered around me, creating a protective shield. My hand opened wide, and a giant portal ripped into the scenery.

In the background, the voices of Fae from every court rose as they called for the long-dormant rounds scattered around the Hallowed Hills. The fairy circles rushed to answer their old masters, cluttering the air.

My Fomorinans moved through my portal. Rounds maneuvered past my portal to glimpse the surface location. The once blue and black building with a wall of glass in Georgia that housed the CDC stood in the distance, yet the sign denoting the building was long gone.

Rounds of all sizes blasted to the surface, leaving a sonic boom behind.

I hummed a protective bubble over myself and the rest of the Fomorians to keep the ear rattling sound at bay. When the last of my guard stepped through the portal, I flashed to the other side and let it slam close with a loud crack.

I didn't care about stealth. That was Mercia's bag.

I'm the blunt instrument. I'm here for war. I'll burn the world down to get to Janice or to kill Jacques. I'm not a hero.

Georgia didn't look anything like I remembered. There were trees everywhere. But what was I expecting? The Fae apocalypse happened a long time ago.

Humanity doesn't bounce back as quick as fairies.

A forest surrounded the complex. Bonn and his court moved into the trees, leaping from one branch to another. Mod's Fae moved into pre-organized locations around old cement highway ties. They were used to reinforce what was left of a fence. They were the first of embattlements around the building.

The sky cracked with new rounds joining us on the surface.

My wings flapped, carrying me up for a birdseye view of the ground. The main building shimmered with a shield. The wake lines twisted together for strength. The witches who cast it were weak, to say the least.

I pulled a fireball into my elemental hand and tossed it at the shield. It slammed into the blockage and pushed through, landing on the dry grass to burn. Within moments, the surrounding field was a flame.

"My Queen," Mod's voice cut through the vision before me.

My head turned to take her in. She held her body erect with the grace of a willow tree, bending with the breeze. She waked with an autumn gold. I waited for her to speak.

"Leave the army here. I have found another way."

It was all I needed. "Show me." I sent a Fomorian to Bonn with a message - *keep them distracted.*

Her round shot toward the forest and a small lake beyond. Keeping on the heels of her round was too easy and forced me to hold back.

The small lake was edged by a reedy bank next to an old road, which led to the CDC. The lake looked man-made. Its shape was too regular, and there appeared to be pipes in the center.

I veered away from Mod and instead inspected the pipes. They formed a circle, and attached to it were nozzles. It was an old fountain used to aerate the water, to keep fish alive and mosquitoes at bay. Many subdivisions had them for lowering the water table at a building site.

When my dad finished with the Marines, he went into construction. He ran heavy equipment, backhoes, and excavators of all kinds. He dug all kinds of job sites in Texas, including lakes.

Rain in Texas comes down hard and fast, sometimes with nowhere to go. A lake can mean the difference between being in a flash flood or having a full lake.

This was one of those. A place to put water in heavy rain. Right now, we were in the dry season. The lake was low.

That brought me back to Mod and her way in. I already understood what it was — drainage. I made my way to the reeds and the culvert running under the road. Mod leaned against the cement side of the drainage pipe.

"I scouted all the way back. It leads to an underground fake stone structure. There are human machines from the before."

I stared off into the darkness. "A parking building," I remarked though I think I was the only person who knew what that meant.

"We can send the entire army through here when the sun rises. The fake stone will protect them from the sun's raises."

I turned to look at Mod. It struck me. That deal, the one for the surface, was made by a human, not a Fae. The proclamation that went with it was made later.

"What did Mabe say when she gave up the surface? The exact words?" I asked.

"I don't know, my Queen. I had not yet hatched."

I stared through Mod for a few moments. "Wait here. I'll be right back." I slammed a portal into the side of the cement culvert.

"But, my Queen, the moonlight will fade…"

"Hold the line around the buildings. Station one group here. No one gets in, and nobody gets out. Got it?" I said and stepped through to the library.

Lavender shot to her feet, "My Queen," she stumbled over her words. The Creeper Keeper dropped a book, revealing the swirled marking up her arm in a faded yellow.

"Tell me what Mabe said when she gave the surface way to the humans!"

CHAPTER 13

MERCIA

The blood tornado moved faster than I ever thought possible. But magic moves at its own pace, and I was barely able to keep up. My ability to flash only worked when I could see where I was going. The blood never stopped.

I caught my breath for a second while the blood continued on.

It was moving west at a steady clip. This was the general path Momma took to my hatching cave. The trees grew thick, and the wakes of magic in the area told the story of a spell to raise the groundwater level. The blood only gave me a second to taste the spell and know it as mine. All those years ago, I enriched this area with my magic.

A smile touched my lips.

The blood made a beeline further on, and I followed. I sang for sixpence and the power it would give me to keep up.

On the horizon, a spire grew. The shape was familiar, and my finding spell was heading right for it.

I felt the iron long before I could assure myself of what it was. The burning of iron can not be denied. The spire turned into an extremely tall structure made of iron and steel.

The blood grew erratic, moving in circles, then stood still.

It didn't need to go beyond the edge of the little town. A clean painted sign told me I was in the right place.

Paris, Texas, pixie shit!

The Eiffel Tower's replica loomed in the distance over the little town.

Momma would never go near that monstrosity.

I stared down the main street at the summitry of the layout. The founders had planned well. What was left of the town were old buildings from the early haydays. In the center of town was what looked to be a park. My nose told me there was more to it than just a few overgrown trees. The horrid iron tower stood alone, surrounded by the leftover concrete and the iron laid down to hold it in place.

It wasn't hard to understand why Momma said not to come here. The iron tower shielded the quilt, and as long as I didn't give its hiding place away, there was no reason why anyone would look here.

The name alone would keep any changeling a quarter or better away.

I kept to the open ground on the outskirts of the town, following the blood trail. Finally, the blood moved into the town proper and stopped over the top of what was left of a fountain. The top portion was broken off sometime in the last fifty years and landed in the main basin. Water still poured from the top of the center post, looking more like a fire hose than a fountain.

The water pressure was a marvel for the world after the fall.

The white marble of the fountain gleamed in the half moonlight. If I was any other kind of Fae, I might have enjoyed the sight of such a beautiful piece of rock. Instead, I ground my teeth down on my latest encounter with another piece of rock — Ignis.

I moved in to search the water feature for the key to Danu's stones and the future of Fae. The humans didn't just install a fountain in the center of a park. No, they turned it into a monument to the town itself.

I snickered and looked around. When the fountain wasn't enough, they built that awful tower of Fae terror. The leftover wakes of Fae magic threaded the countryside where the Fae destroyed the town over that hunk of iron.

The fountain was the apex of a stone pedestal. One could almost pick out the original design of the watery travesty. Chunks of poured concrete from the steps lay randomly as if they were kicked there.

There were no magical disturbances other than the remnants of fifty-year-old magic. I pulled my hunter's cloak in tight to allow the canopy of the trees to keep the moonlight at bay just enough for a closer look.

My feet cautiously toed their way over the cracked roads and into the well-trimmed grass and weeds. It felt wrong.

So wrong.

As I reached the park's old edge, a cement curb lifted up from the road, and my foot froze in mid-air.

The moonlight over the fountain shivered with a gloss and glimmer of a glamor. My mouth opened for a taste of the magic. I pulled it deep into my lungs, using all my senses to find the maker of this spell.

It was a strange flavor of magic laced with the blood of Puca. It was something made from ash, fire, and acorns.

My closed eyes flew open.

Momma.

I moved without thought to grasp the prize, and the magic urged me on, only to smash into an invisible wall. The glamor on the other side dissolved, and the fountain was gone. There was no fresh water, only the shadowy form of a long-dead creature, one I didn't believe ever existed. I'd chalked it up to human imagination and fantasy.

The shadowy creature released an ear-cracking roar and spoke. "Have you come to free me, little hunter?"

The use of Puca's nickname cut me with the same amount of pain as a bone saw.

The creature waddled over to the center of the fountain and swatted at the blood hanging in the air. "Is this how Fae hunt now, with the blood of a King?" It inquired, then batted its claw through the blood its feline nature had taken form.

The beast's personality was a mix between a cat and a mermaid. It listened to no one and liked shiny things. The fountain was full of coins from every metal and country of the old world. It was a dragon's horde.

I wracked my brain to recall if Momma had said anything about dragons, only to come up empty. The human stories said dragons like caves and filled them with their ill-gotten treasure. You couldn't make a deal with a dragon for anything. They would kill you. The only way to get their treasure was to kill them.

How had Momma gotten it here? Where did all the treasure come from? How do I get in?

I was neither a hobbit nor a dwarf. There was no secret passage for me to wiggle through. I could have pulled my hunter's cloak and hide in the shadows to reach the horde, but then what?

If I knew anything about Fae, it was that nothing was as it seemed, and sneaking in wasn't going to work.

I could open a portal, but without knowing where the quilt was in the massive pile, I'd have to dig, and digging takes time.

"Pil said someone would come," the beast offered.

I could take the bait. Momma wouldn't have left me with no way to reach the one item I was left to defend.

Magic isn't impervious, it has loopholes, and it bends.

"Circle, circle, round and round, you'll never reach me on the ground," the dragon laughed. Its throat worked, rumbling out the sounds of the words.

It moved to mirror my steps. "You look like her, the great hunter Pil. She trapped me here to guard for Fae." Its mouth snapped at me. The ghoulish jawbone covered in scales was meant to frighten me. The eyes of the dragon whirled with wyld.

Was it a product of a Wyld King?

A second later, the wheels really began to turn. Its legs were stubbed as if cut off at the knees. His skin was scaled with small round leaves. The horns on his head were spiked and twisted, with small nubs dotting their way to the tip. His wings flexed, opened, and closed, revealing a thin membrane of veins that swirled in circles. He was marked with Fae magic. It was in his blood. This wasn't a creation. I swallowed back the truth of what I was looking at.

This was a King that isn't dead.

"What are you? Who are you?" I asked, pushing as much strength into my voice as I could muster.

If he was the very thing I believed him to be, there was no help here. Only another kind of death.

"You taste my magic. You know what I am. As for who I am, it doesn't matter anymore. Pil tricked us all. She trapped me in my dragon form and then saved me for a rainy day. The same way humans dry meat and put it in a pouch for later."

The bag Momma carried and then didn't.

I racked my brain to remember when she stopped, only to again find nothing.

Momma must have stolen my memories or given me a sleeping potion.

I ignored its comments. If Momma tricked him into guarding the quilt, it was worth it. Momma understood Jacques better than anyone alive, save Puca.

"You're here for the song," it whispered. The end of one of his stumpy legs sprouted toes, at the tip of each toe a sharp claw.

My eyes snapped back to the dragon and its machinations for freedom. "What song?" I asked before I could stop myself.

"The one Danu used to change worlds," his reply froze my blood in its veins. "I've seen the song. Of course, I can't sing it anymore." He looked away. "The magic doesn't answer to dragons. But you could sing." His hope fill demeanor struck me as contrived.

The side of my nose curled up before I could stop it, "What do you want in return for the song?" I asked. I didn't actually need the blanket, only the song.

"Freedom," he remarked and flicked his tail at the shield. As if that was in the cards, to begin with. There had to be more to it. Freedom wouldn't be enough for most Fae, even ones trapped in dragon form. They would want revenge.

"What's your name?"

Names have power.

Without a name, one couldn't bind a Fae to the magic or trap them.

"You are too young to know me. So it doesn't matter." He slunk away from where I stood.

The Fae game of words wasn't new to me, though I was out of practice.

I have been under Puca's control too long.

"How did this Pil trap you?" I asked, continuing my inspection of the outer perimeter.

He spat on the ground. The mass sizzled with the heat of a fire. His wings fluttered open and swept a burst of hot air at me, pushing my hood off my head onto my shoulders.

"You carry the crossbow of Jacques' pet, Pil. How did you get it?" He demanded. Smoke escaped from his nostrils and curled up the side of his face.

Questions with questions.

The Fae only know one game, and I was tired of it. The banter was as stale as a crust of bread next to a plague-ridden body.

"Puca killed her and gave it to me." It wasn't a complete lie. I was only playing with the truth a bit. Scanning the pile of metal in the main basin, my eyes trailed over something that appeared black in the dark of night. It could have been trash, soil, wood, or fabric. Yet the wakes moving away spoke of changelings, many changelings, all with a touch of Fae. They each carried enough to create magic.

It was the baby blue wake that gave the game away. Alice's magic was that color, and she tasted of honeysuckle and soap. The magic tickled at the shield surrounding my dragon foe, and I forced one foot in front of the other.

The magic churned in my belly, demanding I turn back to the quilt and take what my master ordered of me.

"The magic around you speaks of pain and loss. You grow thin from an oath," the creature stated.

I *was* growing thin. The magic ate away at me. There were moments when I could see through my limbs.

"Magic doesn't care if you are in pain or lose anything. Magic doesn't speak," I scowled. I didn't need a lecture from a Fae stupid enough to be trapped by Momma.

"Who did you swear to? Jacques? Puca? Jillian?" The creature asked.

I stopped mid-step. Jillian was dead for thousands of years.

My body turned of its own volition, and I really looked at the dragon. His coloring was of the winter court.

Jillian's court.

I knew who this was. I found a book in one of the many places we stayed. The book was about dragons. The boy had to find one and train it. In the book, the dragons were small, like dogs. I showed Momma one of the pictures, and she mentioned once having killed a dragon.

At the time, it seemed like a lie, a metaphor. She said his name was George, the second King of Fae.

CHAPTER 14

SARAH

The Keeper disappeared into the stacks of books only to

return with a moldy old tome covered in dust and a yellow film.

I raised an eyebrow at her and gingerly took the book with my index finger and thumb, laying it on the nearest table.

"Lavender, read exactly what she said." The walls would record every word leaving nothing out.

"Mabe, the third Queen of Fae, took the throne. Moments after her thorny crown emerged from her pate, she screamed, "The surface will belong to all those not of Fae blood from now until the covenant is broken. Fae will rule the night and humanity the day, neither taking what belongs to the other. Thus will there be peace!" The princes arrived a short while later to greet their new Queen and offer felicitations on her glorious win over her fellow changelings."

My teeth worked the flesh of my lips. The covenant was broken, and we didn't even know it.

Why did Mabe add in the last part? Did she understand humanity all too well?

They would never be satisfied with their simple mortality or lack of magic. As long as humans knew of the existence of fairies, they would hunt us in the same fashion we hunted them.

Only we didn't hunt them. We took changelings for the Queen's search. The rest of humanity we left alone. We killed them, yes. But we didn't take what wasn't freely given.

Every human who ever entered the Hallowed Hills came of their own free will. None of the participants in the Queen's search was human. They were one and all part Fae. Even if the part was so small, it fit neatly in a thimble.

Even my old friend Brad. I finally understood what Deston had meant - we were all part of the Fae search for a Queen. The girl who said she was taken with another girl she hated, Olive, Nick, and me. I stopped.

Arty.

Then it hit me. He was too. If it was just a little tinny, tiny bit, they didn't take him just because of me. He was Fae, in some small way.

Part of me wanted to cry. Because if Arty had just learned a little magic, he could have lived. But he didn't and perhaps never would have. I let him leave, just like all the other changelings from the search.

It hit me hard. I let them all leave. They had knowledge that humanity should never have had access to. I let them leave willingly.

Humanity is harvesting Fae magic via blood. That is taking.

I looked at Lavender, then at the Keeper's hooded figure. "The covenant is broken. Humanity has taken what belongs to us."

"But what do we do about it?" Lavender asked as the wakes around her spoke of a bone-tired soul.

All the time she's spent in the library was wearing on her. She didn't belong here, but in a workroom, creating beauty.

"I want you to gather supplies for a long trip. When this is over, everything is going to change. Pack for me too." I cupped her cheek and gave her a wan smile.

Lavender left in a rush.

"Time is a problem. Shouldn't you return to the surface and the battle?" The oily voice of the creeper keeper asked.

"You have been here for a long time. If the covenant is broken, how do I regain use of the surface during the daylight?"

It was a hope, hope that the keeper would have an answer of some kind. With all these books, I have to believe she was smarter than the rest of us. I'd begun to think of the keeper as a female. At least my gut told me it was a she.

"A proclamation created the covenant. Wouldn't one in reverse suffice?" she moved away from the table, taking Mabe's book with her.

The conversation was over, so I opened a portal to Georgia.

The sky was on fire with magic and projectiles. Before I could get my bearings, a bomb exploded near me, throwing dirt and shrapnel into the air.

I hummed a personal shield and searched the area for one of the Princes. In the distance, the enormous shape of a trebuchet dominated the dark terrain. The wood of the structure was woven from the local trees and laced with magic. The rock ammunition waked with magic and the green of Fae fire.

"Release!" A Fae shouted.

The great siege engine whipped around, flinging the magic rock at the shield protecting the CDC. The rock met the barrier, and the Fae fire swirled over the bubble of safety. The shield cracked and evaporated. The sky filled with iron bullets, all raining down on us. Some defected the assault. Others died.

A moment later, the shield appeared anew. Someone was singing it new with every blow.

In the distance, Wott shouted, "Find her and kill her!" A new projectile hit the shield, collapsing it. Fae flashed over the concrete ties and into the fray on the other side. Dark sanguine blood spurted from the bodies as the Fae moved, searching for the witch casting the shield spell.

The song of war and Fae filled the skies all around, either side working its magic to harm the other. I batted bullets and grenades, angling them away from my army and whatever humans might be nearby. This fight wasn't with humanity as a whole, only the assholes stealing from us.

Us?

I'd said us. I had to finally admit I was one of the Fae, not just some hapless leader sucked into their world. I was always part of these Hallowed Hills. I was never going to be anything else. That was a pipe dream, something little girls imagine when their families suck.

I will never stop being Fae because I always was.

Out there in the dim light were my children. Fae I'd birthed with my song. I gave them purpose and color. They were beautiful, all of them.

I didn't need a bumper sticker announcing my kids' honor roll status to be proud. This was my army, and they were terrifying and beautiful in their battle dance.

A pink Fae moved in with her round to flank me. "My Queen," She was the changeling from Jacques' court and Mod's new recruit - Peddle.

"We have but minutes until the sun begins to crest the horizon."

I whipped to stare her down. I didn't need some freshly hatched Fae-ling telling me anything. Least of all, what time the sun rises.

Mod joined us, pushing the wind to move fire into the trenches, burning the witches and their human followers. "Should I begin the move?" She asked.

"No," I swallowed.

The sky grew brighter by the second. Most of the Fae faltered in their fight. They glanced up, searching for direction. The witches never stopped.

The only thing I could think to sing and get everyone's attention was The Sound of Silence. It was the cover by Disturbed.

I was going to have a good time with this. If I timed it right, the sun would crest as I hit the chorus.

Hello, darkness, my old friend.

My voice carried over the battlefield. I wanted them to hear my words. I wanted silence. I whispered for the sound of silence.

The magic stopped, the area frozen with my compulsion. My body convulsed with the power necessary to hold every person here in place. Sweat formed under my arms, and my wings shook in an unnatural fashion. My hands formed fists to hold the thousands before me.

I needed just a little longer for the sun.

The first ray hit me, and I screamed with the pain of it. The scent of burning hair surrounded me.

"The covenant of Mabe is broken. The humans broke the peace. They took what didn't belong to them. We are here to take it back. Magic belongs to Fae, not humanity." I shouted over the agony of the sun.

A wake rippled out from me, blanketing the land. The power of the sun vanished. A roar worked over my army. I blasted a fireball into the shield.

Whoever was casting missed the beat, and my forces rushed the line. I pulled Silver and took it to the ground, singing vines to hold my victimizes and slashing for the kill. My left hand burned everything it encountered.

Twisting with the onslaught, I killed with one hand and burned the body away with the other. Red blood sprayed from all directions. I couldn't tell if the sky was pink or the blood in the air was coloring the morning light.

The golden light of Earth's star climbed the sky, and I moved forward. For the first time, the sun shone on me in what felt like years. I wasn't going to sneak in and steal Janice away.

I'm not a thief. I'm a Queen. We go through the front door.

CHAPTER 15

MERCIA

Momma, like all Fae, was excellent with twisting words to her best advantage. Calling George a dragon, to me meant he was a tyrant, not an actual dragon.

"How did Pil trick you?" I asked.

He knocked a claw back and forth to indicate a quid pro quo required of the conversation.

"Fine! I will tell you who my master is if you tell me how Pil trapped you," I huffed as if it was really an issue. I didn't care who knew I was sworn to Puca. Every Fae alive owned him one thing or another.

"That is an interesting trade of information. I will make this trade if you tell me who is King also." His large body sat down with a thump, and his tail curled around the fountain's base. He yawned as if readying himself for a bedtime story and not the short, succinct answers I was prepared to give.

"I am sworn to Puca Oberon," I replied.

"And, who is King?" he urged, nodding his massive head to further his point.

"I give, you give." I cross-stepped away from him to a clean line of sight with the grimoire.

He roared a moment before flame erupted from his maw. The shield held the power of fire at bay, though the heat bled through just fine. I hopped back to keep from getting a tan.

"I told you my terms. You will supply for your King."

I threw my head back and laughed. "You wanted quid pro quo. You got it. I asked for one thing. You asked for two. I gave one, you give one. You give me what I asked for, or you'll get nothing more from me." The magic pushed me to take the quilt, my safety be dammed. My bones itched as little bits disappeared to where the magic took its pounds of flesh.

I gulped to keep my hunter's need to chase at bay.

"Jacques took the Queen and me on a hunt. It was to thank us for the birth of his acorn-colored child, Pil," he huffed at the memory. "The creature we were to hunt was a dragon. They lived on the surface in those days." George lifted his head and gazed around, as if seeing the world with different eyes.

"It was a trick, of course. There was no dragon." The rue-laced laugh wasn't lost on me. Jacques was clever. Nick had explained that to me in great detail.

"And—"

"Once I entered the forest, my fate was set. Jacques had a protection bubble over the area. It kept Jillian, my Queen, out and locked me inside." His chest rumbled with the memory. "I never looked back. I never checked on my Queen. That was part of Jacques' plan."

His rue-filled answers didn't tell me what I wanted to know - how Momma got him here; how did she lock him in his dragon form, saving him away for another Fae day.

"Jacques only tricked me. Pil threw the killing blow. She sang a fire spell, and I changed to pass through the flames. While I was in my dragon form, she shot with that crossbow. The blow didn't kill me as it would a normal Fae. I bled to the point of death, but at the moment I walked two worlds, she pulled me back by blasting my body with my blood from the ground. Somehow she sucked the life from it and pumped it back into me." Smoke leaked from his nostrils and floated around us.

The hunter's curse. She used dead blood to fuel him. Something I had never thought of doing. I only use the hunter's curse to heal myself and continue the fight.

Clever.

"What happened after that?" I asked. My eagerness for an answer gave him the upper hand, and he laughed.

"Oh, no, little one. Now you will repay your King with the information I asked for."

"Jacques is King in your stead," I replied.

He threw his head back and roared. Fire blasted the trees overhead, and the flame caught. The grass in the park flashed with flame, turning to embers.

"Jillian told me she would never crown Jacques. She claimed she loved me." Fresh blasts of fire erupted. The bright light reflected off his scales, giving me the cold gray color of the winter court. Jacques was from the autumn one. Jillian was the winter princess at that time.

Interesting.

This was my chance. I opened a portal and stepped out on top of the cache. The quilt waked with the latent magic of the witches in Puca's line. I hugged it to my chest and leaped down from the fountain.

"You think to rob me of my only comfort?" He roared. "You smell of lies and the hunt. I can see wyld lives in you."

A clawed foot smashed the ground before me, blocking my path and my escape. I opened a portal to the other side of the shield and stepped through, then flashed to the opposite side of the street, away from the park and the flame's heat.

"Give me my freedom so I may kill Jacques and his pet Pil!" He shouted. The burning trees illuminated the park, turning it into more of a bonfire.

I stopped mid-stride and turned.

"If I free you, what is to keep you from killing me?" I asked and raised a brow.

"I will swear to you," he replied. Liquid dripped from his maw. Everywhere it landed, the ground blacked as if acid spilled.

Do I want this oath? Should I be the one to wield power over this creature?

He was alive but unable to make magic because he was dead at the same time.

"Do you wish to continue this existence?"

"I have lost track of time. I only live for revenge."

He would kill me if he knew who I was.

I could whistle for Puca. I could let him free this beast, let him be Puca's problem. Instead, I took his offer, let right or wrong be dammed.

"Swear to me, Mercia the hunter, daughter of Arthur the brave and Pilar the greatest hunter of all time. To do all I order and never turn against me or harm myself or anyone under my protection. And I, for my part, I will free you from this living death when Jacques is dead."

His kaleidoscope eyes whirled through the rainbow of colors only a Fae could find, tasting the words of his oath. He shifted on his feet and flicked his tail in that oh so feline fashion. With the lift of his head, he roared.

"I, George, the second King of Fae, swear to Mercia the hunter, daughter of Arthur the brave and Pilar the greatest hunter of all time, to never turn against you or harm you or anyone under your protection till you take me from this evil world." The green Fae light of an oath wrapped around us, and the shield burst.

We both gasped at the change. The magic that held him for so long drifted away.

"Now that I own you. I will tell you my mother was Pil."

He screeched, and his wings whipped open, pulling him high into the sky. "I should kill you!" he shouted. "But the magic holds me back. You are no better than your mother. You tricked me." His body undulated with rage. The march of magic began its task of eating away at him. His resistance hastened the chewing.

"Stop, or the magic will eat you. Pil is dead for a long time now. But Jacques is not. I will give you the revenge you have survived so long for. Let that be enough. Jacques and Jillian broke Fae when they killed Danu. You knew what they were doing. You helped them."

He continued to thrash and roar with rage. "I didn't know until we were on the battlefield, and Jacques ordered us to attack. Jillian kept me out of her machinations," he shouted and gnashed his teeth over the answer. The beating of his wings whipped ash into the air to swirl around our bodies and in my hair and eyes.

"What did you do after? Did you kill Jillian for the betrayal of Danu? Or Jacques? No, you went on a hunt for fun." I spit on the ash-covered ground. The bitter taste was all I could feel.

"I couldn't stop a Queen."

The laugh that came forth was a surprise to me and him, "Why not? Jillian and Jacques did. You're a coward, hiding behind the blood-soaked skirts of Jillian. Well, I'm in charge now, and you would hide behind me. I want you on the battlefield in the vanguard. We are at war. It has been thousands of years since Jack and Jill went up the hill and broke the Fae crown. Jacques is now raising an army using Fae he's killed to turn humans into magic users."

George lowered to the ground, closing his wings. His hot rage went cold with the realization of what he was a party to.

"Your Queen needs you to help stop him. And by Danu, I will make you fix what you stood by and watched break. George, second King of Fae, when I open the next portal, you will go through to the CDC, and we will wage war." I growled at the prey I'd hunted down. He was the biggest prize of all.

He roared in response, and white-hot flame erupted. His dark gray scales gleamed under the surrounding flames. "Yes, master!"

I blasted the largest portal I'd ever seen open onto the side of a crumbling building, and George stepped through with me right behind. Only we weren't on the surface or at the CDC. We were at Puca's cottage.

Pixie shit!

"Stay here!" I ordered. George plopped to the ground, wrapped his tail around his torso, and then yawned.

The door to the cottage was open and vacant of life. Puca had to be here. The magic brought me here to fulfill my quest. All I needed was to hand the grimoire over to Puca and then take my new pet to the fight.

I didn't want to whistle. I squished my eyes closed and rubbed the sleep away, then sang for sixpence, and the magical jolt it dished out. It left an after-taste of sticking your tongue to a battery. I didn't like it. It made my teeth itch.

"Don't burn anything or speak to anyone until I come back," I snapped at the sleeping dragon.

"Where are you going?" he inquired. If I didn't know better, I'd say he was smiling. This was his first time outside in centuries.

"To find Puca and get this over with," I growled.

George chuckled. "I've said much the same thing. Fae is never done with you." He laid his head on top of his tail. At this angle, he looked like a blue-ish gray rock if you ignored the wakes of magic coming off him.

I opened a portal with no place in mind.

Let the magic take me where I need to be.

I stepped through to an empty throne room. In the center sat a well. My eyes locked onto a black and white flower blooming nearby. It was familiar.

I flashed to the plant, and a deep need to touch the peddles enveloped me.

"You must be Mercia," a hooded female stated.

My hand froze a hair's breathe away from the bloom, and all the energy I'd sung for drained away. My eyes gazed from the flower to the hooded female and back again.

Truth is a battle. When it finally hits you, it's a heavy blow you can't defend against. But what to do with the truth is a different story.

She patted my head. Her soft golden eyes crinkled at the edge with age and sorrow.

"I don't remember seeing a flower the last time I was here," I said and waited for the female's reply.

"It's a Queen's flower. Don't touch it, or it will die. Being Queen is such a delicate thing. One blow can end it all, and yet that blow could renew everything." Her words carried a double meaning, as do most words flowing from a Fae's mouth. They are daggers with two edges, both sides just as likely to kill you.

"You came for the song?"

I pulled the quilt from my satchel and spread it over the stone throne. The fabric was only held together by magic. Untouched nature could have taken it many hundreds of years ago.

She pointed to the center, the first square. "There, the song you seek is there."

I leaned in close. The design was a typical Fae swirl, curling in on itself and twisting out to touch the other squares. Tight stitches created the design. The stitches seemed as if nothing more than a needle pulled through the fabric.

"I don't see anything. The words aren't there," I murmured and squinted for a different view. The design was like the swirls in the well cave, curling in on itself and twisting out again. They made no sense to me.

When I finally looked up, the hooded Fae was gone.

The center of the quilt was different from all the rest. It was larger and tightly woven. The fabric was iridescent in nature and somehow stronger than the surrounding material.

I cut the center square away from the rest of the blanket. I didn't need the excess weight. I strode to the Queen's flower. It waked in a way I'd seen before. The truth was what I saw gave all the answers I would find in this room.

I glanced down at the tightly gripped quilt in my hand. It waked with its secret song. I laid it out over the stone throne, and the answer came to me all at once.

It wasn't a song at all but a grouping of sounds, sounds I could see and memorize. It was all I needed.

"Did you find it?" Puca asked and shuffled around the room. He stepped over the rough-cut pieces of the quilt I'd left behind, then threw Fae fire over them.

His face darkened for a moment with a deep sadness before returning to his devil may care attitude. He glanced from the square on the throne to me and back. "Do you have it? Good." He didn't move to touch it or take it.

I waited for his next order with strained patients. It didn't come. He tossed Fae fire onto this piece, too, "Don't tell anyone save Sarah what it is."

The magic released me from the quest. "Can I go now?" I asked. My heart ached. The magic kept the please dancing on my tongue stuck there.

"Yes, go find Nick," he replied.

"What about you? Aren't you coming?"

"No, I have things to do." Puca surveyed the room, touching the effigy of the dead. After that, he waved me off.

I opened a portal to George, "Let's go." Was all I could muster with the butterflies swooping in my belly.

CHAPTER 16

MERCIA

The ground around the CDC was covered in ash and bodies, both blue and red colored the ground. The wakes were a mish-mash of humanity and Fae. Yet, it was the sunlight that I found most shocking.

In the distance, the Queen kicked a warlock in the gut and stabbed another before slicing the first man with her Quicksilver and burning his flesh to ash.

That explained the volcanic taste in the air. Her control over fire burned everything to its base chemicals.

George swooped down and thumped on the ground behind me.

"Master?" he asked.

He managed to sound begrudging even with one word. I smirked. I finally got why Nick always took a pet on the surface. They were oh so helpful. My flittermice friends were just that friends. But a pet, well, George couldn't be called anything else. He wasn't alive or dead.

The scene told me everything. Sarah hadn't made a battle plan. Not to use a pun, but she was winging it and not getting far.

I flashed to her side.

"Bout time you showed up. Did you get it?" she demanded a moment before George flew overhead. "What the fuck? Is - - is that a dragon?"

"Yes, no, I'll explain later," I shouted over the boom of a rocket exploding against a shield. "Yes, I have it. But this fight is going all wrong. You aren't taking any ground." I swatted a human with milk-white eyes away and sang to put him to sleep. Sarah stabbed him with the Quicksilver before he hit the ground.

My nose curled up at her. She didn't need to kill that guy. He wasn't going to wake up for a long time. "Some of these people are entranced," I stated.

Rocks of all kinds flew through the air, pelting witches here and there. A bolder pinned several people to the ground.

From the way Sarah was fighting, I was not sure she was aware of the fact that she was controlling the rocks. "You think you can do better?" she snarled and stabbed another fighter, only to have their shield deflect her blow.

This guy was a warlock, so I pulled the trigger on my bow, and the bolt slipped through his shield and planted deep in his chest.

"There is another way inside. Let George hold them off while I do my thing," I offered, then had to jump out of the way of a magic blast.

"George? That's funny. George *is* the dragon, and you didn't slay it? Figures," she scoffed. "There's a drain by the lake that leads to a parking building."

I smirked at her, "I know. This isn't my first time here." This would be much easier than my trip with Momma. The only reason we made it out that time was because they didn't know how we got in. This time everyone was focused on the front door.

No one will be watching their back.

Sarah's wings opened, and she lifted into the air. "Go! And take someone with you."

"N— " Nick's name dangled from the tip of my tongue. If he was here, I would choose him. "Cernunnos, two hunters are better than one." She pointed at the trees and went back to fighting.

The old hunter fought with the summer court in the trees.

That is where a real predator should be.

I flashed to a clump of live oaks, weaving around skirmishes as I went.

Cernunnos crouched in a tree, high overhead. He loosed two arrows at once, killing two humans without a drop of Fae blood. I flashed my way to a branch over his head.

"Do you intend to kill me?" He asked while tracking his next prey.

"No, I have a hunt that needs two for success. Are you interested?"

He took to his full height. The tree branch didn't dip with his weight.

He must be light as a feather.

"Why would I help you, Daughter of Pil?" his snarl said one thing, the pulse at his neck another. He was thirsty for the hunt.

"Because it will end the standoff. Sarah will never make through the front door without us," I remarked and pointed at the battle lines in the distance. Anyone with eyes could see we weren't making headway. I squatted on the thin branch supporting me to get closer to Cernunnos.

"Your mother tricked me with a hunt once, and it killed me." He knocked and released an arrow, burying it in a witch's eye. His bow carried the sure-shot song. It was laced into all his weapons. A moment later, he started singing, *Come back, Peter, come back, Paul,* and the blood-soaked arrow returned to his quiver to be used again.

"I'm not my mother. I want what Sarah wants, Nick back. Will you come? Or do I need to inform your Queen of your cowardice?" I twisted that knife in an already open wound.

Yeah, he didn't like me. So what? Most Fae looked at me like I was dirt. Being the daughter of the greatest hunter and assassin of all time, along with Jacque's pet, didn't endear Momma to anyone. Other than me, because I didn't care.

"I will attend, but you must walk before me." His response made me want to laugh.

"Yeah, I'll stay where you can see me," I smiled at him, "Only because I'm leading the way. I don't stab people in the back. I hunt them," I remarked, then flashed deeper into the woods, reaching the edge of the lake in time to spot a human patrol.

I whipped my arm out, holding Cernunnos at bay. "Let them pass, or we can put them to sleep. Your choice."

"Sleep? Why? We can kill them and be done with it."

He is going to fight everything I say.

I sighed, "They don't have magic, and killing them doesn't get us anything," I growled and mumbled under my breath, "Pixie shit!"

"Have you ever even seen a pixie?" he whispered as the humans passed by.

"No, but Pil hated them."

"They are blind killers, eating anything in their path," his voice carried a smile.

The humans finished passing the drain and our path to the inside. They almost seemed like they didn't even know there was a battle not far from here. I picked my way through the reeds to the culvert, keeping a close eye on the patrol. They waked with enchantment.

Of course, they are calm. They aren't awake.

The mouth of the culvert was guarded by three Fae males. Cernunnos gave them a nod of acknowledgment. I walked past them deeper into the darkness of the drain. When we were far enough in, I spoke.

"One of you stay behind and guard our backs. The other two, let's go."

"I don't travel with changelings," the Fae sneered at me.

I punched him in the eye and road his body to the ground, then sang for my hunter's vine. It wrapped around his body and gaged his mouth.

"Then I guess you're staying behind?" I remarked.

The others chuckled. When we reached the end of the drain, I snapped my fingers to release the hunter's vine.

"You have made an enemy of that one," one of the males remarked.

I shrugged.

Why should I care? I am never going to be accepted anyway. So why get my panties in a wad over it now?

"He's a killer," the male continued, making Cernunnos laugh.

"So am I." I tossed back to shut his cakehole. All they saw was a changeling.

"She is a hunter," Cernunnos supplied.

A small smile touched my lips. He didn't need to like me, but defending our kind was another story.

We walked in silence, in the darkness of the water system, for what seemed like forever when it came to an abrupt end. The grate over our heads was the only exit. There was a low light source emanating from the space above, and I heaved a sigh of relief.

Nothing had changed in the ten years since I'd come this way.

"Above us is a parking structure. Other than a few old cars from before the fall, it should be empty. Don't let that fool you. Sound carries in those spaces as easy as over water."

Cernunnos adjusted his weapons for stealth and sang the grate out of the way, then waved me up. Because apparently, ladies go first. I rolled my eyes.

He had a right to be distrustful. Momma did that to anyone she left behind. They lived with an abiding feeling that it was a mistake that would be remedied at any moment. That dread was part of the reason, even after all these years.

The hate abides. Good.

I needed them to see me the same way. It was the only way Fae would respect me.

I smirked and pulled myself into the cement underground parking structure. The scene was much the same as I remembered. The remains of cars and trucks littered the structure. I couldn't recall whether they were as picked apart as the partial frames I saw now. However, that didn't matter.

There were more. Lots more. And all the new vehicles were Gov issued. Hummers and Jeeps. I only knew what they were because of the names on their backs.

Humming for a car only made sense if you could wield magic. Yet humanity had used these machines well before the fall. Each device carried a small touch of rust here and there. The colors were all the same, a variety of greens mixed together.

The color would be more effective in a forest in summer than an underground parking garage.

The wakes told me we were alone and the machines were cold. Yet, my ears told me the next level was another story. The rumble of an engine echoed in the cavernous space.

"They are readying for an evac. We need to move," I stated in such a low voice no one save a Fae could make out.

Cernunnos flashed over the rungs and onto the cement floor. The other two followed.

I tossed a glamor over myself and turned around as we walked toward the idling engine on the upper floor. My brow cocked at the rest of my party, hoping I wouldn't need a battle chart to point out the obvious.

Cernunnos glamored, but I was not impressed. The glamor was barely human.

I swirled my hand over my face in the air, "Try again."

The other two provided glamors. They sucked just as much. I shook my head and hummed one of my own over each of them.

At least now they look human.

They were dressed as a Gov and not a CB rat.

If these Govs look anything like the ones at the Tower, we'll blend in.

The back of my neck tickled. I couldn't get around the nagging feeling that took over every time I glamored. I always thought that someone would see through the magic, and I'd be dead. It always started as a tickle and slowly turned into a full blow itch.

I stopped walking. We weren't in the right formation, and Govs moved in a certain way. Cernunnos huffed. I ignored it. He tasted the hunt, and I was standing in his way. Though his eagerness boiled just under the surface, the predator in him waited.

Without speaking, I moved each male into the proper position for a Gov squad. I stared them down in turn and swirled my finger. This could get us somewhere fast.

If we keep cool.

"No singing without my say so. Even humming will give us away. I lived among humans. They have a sixth sense about us, and any out-of-place shit will set them off. Especially since we are shitting right over their heads."

They didn't reply, which was fine because I didn't want to hear it. I just hoped none of them had the Fae arrogance to underestimate humanity too much.

That will get us killed.

We took the rise to the next level. This floor opened onto a group of hummers all lined up for evac. I glanced them over, searching for Nick or Ron. Janice would just be the extra bit I needed to finish this. Whoever was in the machines was human. There were a few fake Fae, witches/warlocks. Their wake lines were easy to spot now that I knew what I was looking at. The colors were all primary. There was no special shade, not like a natural Fae. We came in every color there could ever be and then some.

I wasn't just looking for Nick. I was looking for Larka. That piece of pixie shit needed to die. My glamor went from an itch into full-on burn mode. I swallowed back the rage lingering in my throat. I couldn't lose it, not now, not when I was so close to Nick and Ron.

The witches down here were weak. Their magic was fresh and new, as if they'd just received their first treatment. I moved to double time our steps as the first witch spotted us.

When we were close enough, I snapped to attention, and the others followed. She didn't wear any insignia, but that didn't mean she wasn't in charge down here.

"What was your squad doing on Level B7?" The woman asked. She stood ready to act if we didn't give a good answer.

"Looking for a filter on one of the Vs," I replied and pulled a piece I'd taken off from one of the hummers below. I turned it this way and that.

"Who's your commanding officer?" She inquired, taking a deep breath.

Shit!

I didn't know anyone here, so I said the one name I did know. "Major Willis,"

Not everyone knows he's dead even after this long.

Momma killed him just before she died in Paris. It was not just a long shot. It was a not ever gonna work shot.

"Major Willis? Never heard of him. Where's he stationed?" The wakes around her changed, and the taste of soda pop tickled my nose and tongue. The bubbles in that type of drink gave me belching gas, and I didn't like them. They also made me sneeze.

With a quick count around the caravan before me, I guessed there were 20 plus humans and seven witches.

These are not good numbers.

"North, I can't say where," I replied.

The one thing Cassidy taught me was never reveal anything if you don't have to.

Act as if it's all a very important secret, and you will kill for it.

"Don't give me your *hush, hush* bullshit. Tell me what you were really doing down there, or I'll sing you into the next generation," she bared her teeth as part of her threat. Meanwhile, her heart rate jumped to the next floor, while the pheromones that came off her tasted of fear.

This was a flavor I was familiar with. The fear virus flavored everything for me these days.

I glanced left and right, then back to the witch, and leaned in, "Not here," I replied.

She pivoted on one foot, headed for a door, and we followed. The door led to an elevator space, and she pushed the up button.

Inside, I smiled. Leading us to a private space was all I needed her to do. The door dinged, and we moved into the box I kept her in front of me. Only as we stepped through to the elevator the glamor was stripped away.

I shoved her into the back wall, then retched her around and punched her in the face.

"Stop the door!" I ordered, and the cardinal red-eyed male thrust his hand out just in time.

"Where are Nick and Ron?" I demanded.

The witch's eyes rolled around in her head for a moment before she blinked and focused on me. "Two floors up."

Her reply bothered me. I knew there were seven subfloors, all part of the parking structure. We were on six. Two floors up meant only four.

Why keep them on a parking floor?

"You're lying." I punched her in the chest, forcing all the air out of her lungs. She wasn't well trained. Her magic reflexes were almost none existent. We got lucky. "Take us to them, or I'll use magic to cut you apart one chunk at a time."

"The Queen has a hand of fire. She will burn you and leave you alive long enough to heal, then start all over again," Cernunnos stated.

The red male fingered her hair with a devilish grin. Whatever he was thinking, rape wasn't part of my information extraction plan.

The woman whimpered. "You're the changeling they've been looking for? Mercia?" She remarked.

"Now you're getting it. Yes." I pulled a dagger from my leather vest and traced it along her throat. "So, you know what I'm capable of?" My other fist slammed into her side again, knocking the air out. I nodded, encouraging her to nod with me, "I kill everyone who gets in my way." My rep was long and, at times, helpful.

Her whimper turned into a watery meltdown. The liquid flowed from every opening as she emptied her bladder onto the floor. My nose turned up at her.

"Subfloor 3. No one's allowed on that floor, and the elevators won't stop there."

"Camden, push the floor below that one," Cernunnos said.

Camden? I guess everyone needs a name.

Though as far as names go, that one sucked. He hit the button, the doors closed, and our box lurched up. I hummed a shield over the witch and entranced her. Then opened the roof hatch to the moving box.

"Help me hide her," I remarked.

Camden sang C*ome back, Peter, Come back, Paul* and floated her through the opening onto the elevator roof. We followed right behind.

No way I'm letting the doors open, and us be fish in a barrel.

CHAPTER 17

SARAH

Mercia disappeared into the forest along with her promises. She was right. We weren't making any headway. I'd rushed in without a plan, and we were getting nowhere fast. At least not fast enough. Bonn and Wott had their people lined up in some fashion and were pushing back.

Yet Mod and her court couldn't grab an inch. The winter court was dying left and right. I sang for them to rally to me. Now would be a great time to have Janice's judging eyes staring down at me. At least he was the Minister of War for the winter court and knew how to command them.

"We need to keep all eyes out here on us." The debris flying through the air came to a halt. I looked down at my left hand. The burning embers were barely held in check under the skin. I moved my hand up into the air, and the rocks moved with me. My teeth dug into my lower lip as I bit it.

The power of fire comes with control over the minerals in the soil and rocks. My hand closed into a fist, and some of the rocks exploded. The cold weather Fae stared at me with ice-filled eyes. Some were so cold they carried no color at all, just the white-ish blue of snow left too long to its own devices.

I pulled some of the rocks to us and held them over our heads. "Sing and take control of these rocks. I will bring more. When the shield comes down, you attack with song and stone. I give you the use of fire, each and every one. Don't waste your life needlessly."

The crowd murmured. Small flames sparked all around. The court spread out before me, covering the barrier sections allotted to us. The shield fell, and the cold of winter descended. I watched as witches and warlocks burst into flame with a fireball. Stones collided with bodies and crashed into barricades. It only took a few seconds, but the shield caster was gone, and my army moved forward.

The pulse in my throat leaped at the idea that Janice was just on the other side of a door, not far from where I stood.

The hopium works like a drug.

I searched the bodies for some sign that even one person had contact with Janice.

Jacques would never allow that.

It was stupid, and I had to force myself to stop.

Jacques was in that building somewhere. Thinking you're ready and reaching the point of readiness were totally different things. Big talk only works if you can back it up.

Most of the CDC above ground were nothing more than glass windows. I sang for Annie Lenox, and with her, *It feels like walking on broken glass*, every window burst.

After that, I threw a shield over the building keeping the glass inside and whatever magic the witches were using at bay. That was when the real problems began.

Something whizzed past me, grazing my arm. I whipped around to catch a glimpse of it. It was a bullet, and it waked with iron. I gulped, then shouted, "They are shooting iron!" I used the magic to push the sound of my voice as far as magic would carry my message.

A war cry rose from far off in the distance. The sky clouded and then split to release the heavy burden of rain. The power of water can wash away entire cities. The magic lining the clouds whispered of an element. The Spring court was closely affiliated with Aqualis.

She must have joined the fight.

I searched for my fellow elements. However, there was no sign. Aqualis was the first to join me and my opposite in the circle of destruction. I still felt a kinship with her. We were opposites who didn't oppose each other.

My people flashed to the front door and flooded into the building. A winter Fae moved to block my entry. "My Queen, we must check for your safety."

"You no stand-in Queen's way," The Fomorian leader, Balor, barked. He bared his teeth at the Fae and rolled his one shoulder, readying for a fight.

"I'm not waiting in the back like a child." I pushed the Fae back. "I'm the tip of the spear. Take my right side and follow a real leader."

The tip of the spear.

My dad always said that whenever he had to leave, the Marines sent him over to what he called the sandpit. I'd never seen a spear until I reached the Hallowed Hills. The Fae fought with them. Only then I understood what dad meant.

The tip is thrust into the battle. First, it is sharp and deadly. The spear reaches deep behind the enemy's defenses to pierce their heart before they can land a blow.

As I flashed through the front door and into the fray, the winter Fae moved to my right and behind me. Bodies of Fae and humans lay on the ground everywhere. The space was a riot of wake lines and magic trails. None of them belonged to Jacques, Janice, or Nick.

I used my compulsion to force witches, humans, and Fae alike out of my way. A bullet ricocheted off the wall near my head. My eyes followed the iron path back to its shooter, and I flashed to his side and slashed him from stem to stern.

The old me would have held back. That me was a child and believed she was human. The other me understood you couldn't operate in this new world like that.

A barrage of iron raced down the hall at me, and I used my magic and batted them out of the air and forcing them into the nearest wall.

A woman with white hair appeared. Her dark skin and light eyes told me who she was. Nick's description left out how pretty she was.

Larka.

She sang for *Mary and her lamb*. I pulled that spell from her and crushed it in my hand. In reply, I threw Queen's *Who wants to live forever* at her. The magic raced down the hall. Her eyes widened, and she dove through an open door. The magic smashed into a warlock standing nearby and withered him to dust.

There can be only one, and it wasn't him.

From around the door jamb, Larka's voice carried her song and the magic that formed from it. It was a nursery rhyme I'd never heard before. Something about heather and mountains. It sounded Scottish, but then she reached the kicker.

It was cold on that mountain.

A whirlwind of artic cold rushed down the hall. It was enough to engulf everyone in the building beyond me. I raised my left hand and let the fire do its work. Heat radiated from my palm, melting the metal holding the drop-down ceiling. The ceiling tiles caught fire, and smoke filled the hall.

I pushed the power of air at Larka, fanning the embers of fire into flames. The hall burst into an inferno.

"Sarinha," Aquilis' watery voice joined me in the hall and doused the fire, eliminating the threat.

We coughed over the acidic air, and I used the air to push the smoke from the buildings.

Larka was gone, leaving the hall lined with charred bodies all the way to an elevator door.

"Where are your sisters?" I asked Aqualis.

"They will join when the time is right," she remarked with a smile, slicking her damp hair back from her face as if squeezing excess water from the locks. Aqualis placed a finger on her lips and kissed the tip. The water on the floor flowed back to its source, leaving only the dead and charred remains of the hallway.

My wings shifted on my back. The muscles cramped, holding them close to my body. This was the longest I'd gone without flying since they erupted from my spine.

I flashed to the elevator door and used my magic to pry it open.

Janice is here somewhere.

The shaft was lit and a whole lot deeper than I ever believed. It was like a movie where it just kept going. I counted lights. There were twenty or more.

Mod said the tunnel led to a parking floor, so at least a few of those had to be parking only.

Then why have a huge parking lot out front?

It didn't matter now. The reasoning for the parking was gone along with the world that built it. I knew that. It seemed just the other day and yet a lifetime ago. Being inside this building was fucking with my head. It lulled me into the past as if the fall had never happened.

I slapped myself to snap out of it, then turned to my people. "Have we captured anyone?"

The Fomorians shook their head and stared down. My winter Fae showed hands and shook heads. "Then get someone! We need to know where to go."

The grinding of gears and the push of air informed me the elevator was moving. On the other hand, my eyes told me they were headed this way.

I stared down the shaft. There was a body that waked with Fae magic laying on top of the elevator. A moment later,

Mercia pulled out of the hatch in the roof and stood up. She tilted her head back to stare up the shaft. Her eyes locked on me. She threw me a salute. I returned the maneuver.

"What floor?" I shouted.

"Subfloor 3. There are more labs on Sub 6--."

I didn't let her finish. Stepping off the edge, I opened my wings enough to float down. Mercia sang for Jack to make me light as a feather. My feet drifted down and touched to join her.

Cernunnos climbed out of the hatch and smiled. "Sarinha, are the upper floors clear?"

"I don't care. I'm here for Janice," I remarked.

It came out harsh. Cernunnos gave me a sharp nod. I wasn't trying to be a bitch, but well, I was.

The elevator stopped, and Mercia and another Fae pried the door to the upper floor open. As soon as it was wide enough, I flashed through the opening into the bright white light of a security door and glass windows looking out into a lab filled with bodies. All were deathly white from blood loss.

CHAPTER 18

MERCIA

The Queen was bigger than she looked. The roof barely had enough space for me and my crew. I didn't count on having a flying Fae in my squad. But oh, well, improvise—that's what hunters do.

Camden and I pried the doors open, and Sarah jumped through as soon as it was wide enough for her hips to pass. Her wings tightened against her back as she moved.

I have to admit it was cool.

I didn't want wings, but they were badass.

I jumped through the opening in time to see all the tempered glass in the lab shattered and sprayed everywhere. I shielded my body to keep the micro-cuts from bleeding my strength away.

Sarah blasted the doors open, alerting everyone on this floor of our position.

Pixie shit!

"I know you're Queen and all, but there is no reason to inform the entire floor we're here," I shouted at her.

She turned and scowled at me, "They already know, for fuck sake. I've burned half the building already, so keep your pantie hose on." She turned to the first witch that emerged and shot her point-blank in the chest. The bullet went straight through and exploded out the back, ripping a huge hole in the witch's chest.

The light in her eyes died, and her blood sprayed everywhere.

It dawned on me that if I had the red ring, I could have pulled the magic from her and left her alive. Sarah was more Fae than human if she had any humanity left.

"You don't have to kill them all," I shouted.

"I'm here for two reasons and only two reasons. Janice and Jacques, everyone else is fodder," she returned.

The wakes around her spoke of heartache. Her coloring was a muddy brown. She was not handling this as well as I was.

"And Nick," I added.

She huffed, "Yeah, him too."

I couldn't argue with her. I was here for a few reasons myself. Jacques was lower on the list, but he was there.

The tables around the room were cloaked in plastic sheeting, and the bodies were cut open at hips and shoulders. Some of the bodies looked like they had stitched them up, and allowed them to heal, only to cut them open again for a new batch.

I petted the hair back from a girl's face. She was barely sixteen. Not even fully grown in human years. Her magic was so weak it was a joke to even take it. Before I could stop myself, a green flame of Fae grew in my hand and placed it on her chest.

The magic quickly took back what belonged to us, and her body was gone. The flame went out. I looked up to find a man in a white coat laced with magic, cowering under the next table. My feet stomped over to him.

I grabbed him by the neck and drug him out of his hiding place. A roar grew in my chest and erupted from my mouth. I slammed his body into the ash left behind by the girl.

"Where is he? Where's Nick?" I shouted.

Phantom pain bloomed in my hip. All I could hear was the high pitch whine of the drill as it hit my bone and began to dig.

The man's face turned red as he gasped for air. I released his throat. "Talk!" I yelled.

"He isn't here."

I punched the side of his head, knowing it would make him see stars but not impair his ability to speak, only organize his thoughts. "Try again!"

He coughed, "Maybe on another floor. We only extract the bone marrow." His bladder chose that moment to join the party. The scent of ammonia laced urine filled the air, gaging me. The crotch of his protective suit darkened with dampness. The liquid found its way off the table and dripped onto the floor.

"What's he got?" Sarah asked.

"Nothing so far," I sang to enchant him and asked again. But no matter how many ways I asked, he'd never seen Nick, Janice, or Jacques. He'd never even given anyone a bone marrow treatment. He was just the chop shop man.

His whole job was to bleed children dry. My nostrils flared as I worked to hold back nausea. I was tired, and he looked like a nice snack.

I cut his chest open and pushed my hand up under the ribcage. I gripped his heart and sang for the hunter's curse. His cheap, weak magic tasted of dirty water fished out of a shallow stream taken not far enough from humanity to be fresh. I spit the taste on the floor as his body turned into a hollowed-out husk.

Sarah looked from him to me.

"What? Like you've never sucked magic away before?" I asked, wiping my blood-soaked hand off on the guy's white coat and pushed past her.

She didn't get it. She had probably never been used like that before.

"Yes, I have. Cernunnos used a red stone on me and every other contender. I took my magic back. It's a dangerous power," she remarked.

I burst out laughing, "Boy, are you telling me?" I shook my head. I moved around the lab and then into the next one. I searched the entire floor. There was no sign of Nick or Ron.

I moved to the elevator shaft and pushed the button for the box. This floor was a waste of time, as was every floor in the building. Sarah killed every witch she encountered, and I entranced every human and sent them on their way with a ten-day spell release.

They didn't all need to die. Sarah didn't ascribe to that mindset. She thought if they were here, they were guilty. She didn't understand how the surface worked after the fall. Most people didn't have many choices. She didn't see what I saw - the beds in rooms with locks. Most of these lab people were prisoners just as much as the changelings they worked on.

It was all so fucked up that my nervous energy forced me to vomit three times. I killed a few more warlocks. They knew what they were getting into. They agreed to the treatments.

The offices were above ground and just as empty as the labs. Sarah burned computers and hard drives, whatever those were, on sight. She didn't want anyone repeating the research here.

That is a plan I can get on board with.

But Nick wasn't here, and my hunter's sense told me he never was. As much as I looked around for a sign of Nick, there was nothing. He would have shifted to a wolf and left at least one hair somewhere.

My chest hurt. Frustration welled up inside me, only to slowly be replaced by despair.

"We found her glamored in an office bathroom on the top floor."

The announcement ripped me from the melancholy that I had slipped into.

The white hair witch on the floor lifted her head to stare me down. A smile played over her face a moment before my fist slammed into her nose, cracking the cartilage.

CHAPTER 19

SARAH

The white hair of the woman on the floor left no doubt of what side she was on. Jacques had people everywhere, and I hadn't bothered to stop him. My belief that being Queen was enough to quell anyone working on his behalf blinded me.

Mercia cracked her in the face, "Larka!" Mercia stated with disdain. The hate waking off her was enough to choke anyone.

As she lay tied on her side, I noticed that the woman's belly had a superficial cut across it. I pushed her into a sitting position. Her response was to laugh at us. "They aren't here and never were." Larka lifted her chin in defiance, "I knew Cassidy would tell you everything to save his own skin. What a piece of shit. He was never a true Warlock. We only used this place as an axillary location. To trap YOU."

She stared Mercia down.

She saw Mercia as the biggest threat. That was interesting.

"Everyone is prey to someone else," Mercia growled.

"I don't feel trapped," Mercia laughed, "Hunters sense these things." She scrunched her nose for emphasis. "But you wouldn't understand that. All your magic was stolen." Mercia moved in close to Larka and sniffed, then spit on the floor. "Disgusting! You smell of innocent blood. How many kids did you murder after Cassidy explained how he became a Warlock?"

"They didn't matter. We needed to defend ourselves from her and all of her kind." She pointed a finger at me. She had no idea that I grew up human.

"You are part human. You should get that." Her eyes were narrow and shifting.

Even she didn't believe her own bullshit. She was hoping to turn Mercia against us.

What a foolish plan.

Mercia, from what I could tell, couldn't be turned by anyone.

"I wouldn't kill kids to get what I want," she yelled. Her finger clicked the crossbow's trigger before I could stop her. The bolt sank into Larka's shoulder, and a scream filled the office space.

I pulled Silver from its scabbard and set the tip on the base of the bolt in her should. I gave it a little push, making her cry out.

"Do you know about Quicksilver?" I asked.

Larka scowled at me, replying through gritted teeth, "Yes."

"Good. Then you know it will kill anyone not fully Fae. For instance, someone like you," I remarked. Her hard eyes widened with deep fear.

"It wouldn't take more than a paper cut, and the Quicksilver would do its work. Have you ever seen someone die from a Quicksilver blade? I know Nick used one at the bridge. Did you see it?" I asked.

She tilted her head down and then up with slow understanding. The blood in her dark skin drained away, leaving her ashen and desperate.

"It won't matter what song you or anyone else sings. Once the blade breaks the skin, you will die." I whispered the hard truth I'd learned in the forest as I watched the fake Nick die.

Mercia moved back and began pacing the room. A growl issued from her chest. Mercia didn't have the self-control Puca and Nick did.

If she loses it, this will be all over. She'd shift into a wolf and tear Larka apart. I was only toying with Larka. Mercia wanted to kill her and be done with it.

"Tell me where Janice and Nick are. Where is Jacques? He left you here knowing I would find you and kill you. That's what happens to Jacques' minions, one and all." I stared her down.

"I'm not his minion. We're allies!" She shouted. It was clear that even she didn't believe that anymore. It was nothing more than a lie she told herself. I could see how the domino of mistakes played behind her eyes.

"The only one who always survives is Jacques," Mercia remarked with a bitter laugh.

"If you promise not to use the Quicksilver on me, I'll tell you where they are."

Mercia threw her head back and laughed. "She even tries to deal like a Fae." Mercia kicked the woman in the back, then pulled a dagger, flipped it in the air, and grabbed it with the intent to begin cutting. Larka lurched to the side and slumped on the floor.

I put my hand up, stopping Mercia in place. "I promise not to use the Quicksilver blade on you, only if you tell me where Jacques, Nick, and Janice are," I stated.

"De-trick, some old army base up north," she supplied. The wakes around her confirmed the truth of her words. "From before the fall. It's where the Govs are."

Mercia whistled, then sang *the worms go in, the worms go out*. Just like that, an old map of the US formed in the air. It was marked with cities and roads.

I didn't need the map. I knew where Fort De-trick — Detrick was. The US Government had labs there. Back in the days, they used to house the deadliest pathogens known to man there. It made sense.

Humanity was being attacked. Why study your enemy at the CDC? It was under civilian control. Detrick, on the other hand, was nuclear-hardened for an attack. They just didn't plan on magic.

"Mercia, when Pil found the major guy who killed Arty, where were you?" I opened my hand and pressed down on the air. The move pushed Larka to the floor, giving her enough room to breath but not enough to sing.

Mercia pointed to a place on the map, "Merry-land,"

I snorted. I couldn't help it. "Maryland, not Merry-land. It was named after a Queen named Mary."

"That's what I said," Mercia huffed and sneered at me.

She looked so much like Arty when he stumbled and that twisted my heart. "Merryland it is. Let's get the troops and go."

"Can I kill her?" Mercia asked and hooked a thumb over her shoulder at Larka.

"No, I have a better plan."

She huffed again as if I was taking all her fun away. My left hand flared at her lack of respect. I pushed the need to burn back into the little bottle I needed to keep it in and turned back to Larka. With a closed fist on my right hand, I aimed the red stone ring at Larka.

Mercia announced, "For all the children you stole their lifeblood from just so you could have magic… I hope you burn from the inside out!" She spat on the floor, then smiled.

Mercia was going to enjoy this as much as I was. Magic was never meant for her kind.

The ring struck like a viper. It dug its magic fangs into Larka's bones and sucked out the marrow that didn't belong to her. The magic waked over the room in time with her beating heart. Her heart rate shot through the roof, and she screeched in agony.

"It hurts when someone sucks your magic away, doesn't it?" Mercia yelled over the wailing woman.

Larka's hair turned from the white of Fae to the gray of an old woman. Her face wrinkled with age and time. That rounded bloom of youth all Fae enjoy slipped away with every draw of the ring.

Her light eyes turned back to the natural black dictated by her DNA until there was nothing left but an old human woman. Tears streamed down her face as she blubbered.

Mercia leaned down and got in her face. "Where is Ron? What did you do to him?" she hissed.

Larka didn't answer. Snot dripped out of her nose and over her full lips. She sniffled and blinked as she looked up at us.

"Your little friend is dead. We killed him after we caught Puca's son. We didn't need him as bait anymore. We had your lover. He wasn't Fae. What good was he?" She asked. Her human eyes spoke of innocence, but I knew better. She was evil, with or without Fae blood. She killed kids.

I glanced at Mercia and handed her my sword.

Larka's lips trembled. "You said you wouldn't use the Quicksilver on me."

Mercia smirked, "I didn't say anything like that. Part of being Fae is the art of the deal. When a bargain is struck you better make sure you covered all your bases. You didn't ask for *my* promise." A low rueful chuckle issued from her lips.

"But—" sputtered Larka as Mercia landed the first blow using a dagger. Part of her one good arm dropped to the ground, sounding like a large tree branch hitting the soil. It was the very human scream that followed. I turned away from Mercia, and her blood-covered dagger.

"Where is his body?" Mercia yelled. Her blue eyes glowed with rage as fur formed on her neck and hands.

Larka wailed while Mercia sliced another pound of flesh out as the slow march of death moved over her body. Her old flesh was so sunken, to begin with, it wouldn't take as long as Nick did in the bubble. Mercia was drawing her death out by waiting to use the Quicksilver.

The vision sickened me, and Nick wasn't here. Neither was Janice, and it turned my insides. At least I had the hope of life. Mercia's friend was dead. The hunter in her couldn't take the loss.

Mercia lifted the blade, "Every cut makes death come a little faster."

Larka sobbed, "We burned him." Mercia stabbed her in the foot between two toes.

I left the room. Mercia was going to torture Larka until all her demons were gone and what little the woman knew was ours. I didn't want to stay and watch. I had my own demons to slowly kill.

CHAPTER 20

MERCIA

I rubbed Larka's blood from my face. It felt tainted. That feeling was in my head, yet I couldn't shake it. Cassidy told her how to steal magic, and she did. I wondered how many died before she was successful?

Ron was gone. I failed him. He was my first friend and the only person who ever stuck their neck out for me, and I got him killed. The guilt bowed me down. My heart grew heavy, and the oh, so human tears pricked at my eyes. The leather of my sleeve wasn't absorbent, yet I rubbed it across my face anyway. Outwardly, it appeared I was wiping the blood, not tears, away.

Larka's curly gray hair was speckled with both red and blue blood. Her withered body was hardly worth the trouble I worked over it.

I wanted to go find the incinerator and shift through the ashes for Ron's bones. No matter how many times I kill, it won't bring Ron back. I can't let that happen to Nick. Instead, I looked at Sarah. I wanted to see what she was going to do next.

Sarah pointed up and left the room. She could find her own way to Detrick. I was going there under my own speed.

I ripped a portal open on the blood-splattered wall and stepped through to Merryland. The gray sky belied any belief that this place was merry in any way. The trees were leafless and black, brown, or gray.

It is anything but merry.

I hummed, *the worms go in, the worms go out,* and Momma's map appeared before me. The place Sarah had indicated lit up along with my location. The proximity was minuscule. I could flash there in no time.

Jacques would be expecting Sarah and an army. He knew I would come for Nick. The only outlier was George.

George swore fealty to me, but he wasn't Fae anymore. I took the chance that magic considered him a pet and snapped my fingers as I would for any animal I'd entranced.

The air remained still and damp with cold. I didn't know what I expected. For George to appear? He was a one-time King.

But Kings that die lose their abilities.

Cernunnos didn't have his. George was only trapped as a dragon because that was the form he chose before Momma killed him.

She tricked him into a change. Part of me admired Momma. Her ability to turn any situation to her advantage was a marvel.

Even in death, she, and now I, have the upper hand in this fight.

Jacques didn't know about George, and that was my play.

The humans at Detrick would piss themselves in fear. The witches would too. Jacques and Janice are the only two who might not shoot pixie shit on themselves. That was the upper hand I needed.

A roar broke the sound barrier in the distance. Flame tore the sky-high in the clouds. A moment later, George's heavy gray body landed nearby. He huffed, "Master?"

"That was fast!" I marveled.

He didn't reply. Maybe he didn't know how fast he could travel? He was in that bubble for a long time.

I wonder where Momma kept him before that.

"Just because I'm as curious as a brownie… where did Momma keep you for all those years before the fountain?" an idea was forming, and my dragon pet was an integral part of it.

"Darkness, Pil, kept me in darkness. She folded my form into a small bag. I sat for many ages undisturbed in darkness. Every so often, the bag opened, and light shone into my black world. The only the far-off sounds indicative of a tower room. Pil rarely spoke to me or anyone else. That is until she brought a man to her rooms. Arthur."

My inspection of George and his form froze. The diamond-shaped head was angled down to stare at me. He was gauging the impact of his story. "Is this your father? You stopped moving at the mention of his name."

I didn't reply. Vassal or no, he didn't need to know that.

"Changeling?"

"Shut the fuck up! I was born from a chrysalis, as all Fae are. I have no father. Only magic!" I shouted.

He chucked, "As you say, your mark of Fae is true. Though I have never seen a Fae with two colors tracing their skin."

It didn't matter what he thought. I was from both worlds. I was Fae, yet I chose humanity as my cause.

Humans suck, but the Fae are so much worse.

"Stop talking about pixie shit. We have work to do." A magic boom ripped the air a couple miles away. I knew that sound. It was the sound of a portal tearing space apart and piecing it back together.

"We don't have a lot of time before Sarah attacks Detrick. I need to get inside before all Cernunnos breaks loose, so lower your shoulder and lift your leg. We're going for a ride."

The gray beast obeyed my request, and I planted my foot in the ridges of his body, climbing to his back. I was seated on a ridge where his neck met his spine. It was as good as it was going to get. I hummed my hunter's vine, and it climbed up the sides of the dragon to curl around my legs and waist. I changed the hum to a song and detached the vines from their earthly anchors to intertwine under George's belly, creating a saddle.

"I have never been ridden like a beast of burden," he remarked. Just under the surface was a bitterness I could understand. I wouldn't want to be treated this way by my greatest enemy's child, either.

"You are not a beast. You are a one-time dragon King. I am lucky to be your master. Now fly."

He huffed smoke over my words, and the great wings behind me lifted and lowered, raising us into the sky. His back shifted, and my vines loosed.

A squeak escaped, and I hummed the vines tighter, adding a new anchor around his neck to keep me from sliding off.

"What is our destination, master?" He was attempting to sound meek, yet everything came out sharp. He was barely able to hold back.

"George, do you want to kill Jacques?" I asked, knowing the answer.

"For all the magic in the Hallowed Hills and the stone throne, yes. I live for no other reason, master."

"Then stop fighting me and your oath. Because we are about to head to Jacques' lair, and you may attack at will after I jump ship. Don't let the magic eat you first."

He tilted his head back and released a blast furnace of flame. The heat pushed my hair back and slicked my body in sweat.

After that, he flew in the direction I indicated. I sang a clouded glamor over the both of us, hoping we blended in with the gray of the sky. George flashed with a speed like I'd never dreamed. Nick said humans had the ability to break the sound barrier at one time. George moved so fast I was not sure my screams could keep up with us.

When he finally stopped, we were hovering over a base of some kind. The buildings were well ordered as if the fall had never touched here.

This is it.

"Circle around, flying as low as you dare. I want a good look at the layout," I ordered. My vision darted around, taking in every detail. George turned to the side and glided on one wing before beginning the lazy circle of the fort. There were humans everywhere.

Housing for families.

Most were normal, going about their daily lives, unaware of the death floating just over their heads.

George's chest rumbled, sounding like lightning.

"Keep it down, you big oaf," I whispered and patted his neck to let him know I was kidding.

"I have never been an oaf, my master," he bit out.

"It's a joke, for fuck sake."

He didn't respond. I guess he didn't get the joke. It's okay. I didn't laugh at them often either.

When George was finished with the wide circle, he came to a halt over the main gate. The sun was sinking low in the sky, and my chance to get in undetected was sinking with it. The main gate leads through the housing sections. Small houses surrounded the entire fort. There were fortifications all around the outside, capable of defecting an attack from the ground. They assumed whoever was coming would walk.

Fools.

Fae would fly, leap, and secret to enter this stronghold.

I urged George to follow one of the roads past all the living quarters to a second gate. This divided the smaller houses from larger ones. The large homes were well cared for. There were only a few of them. This section was more of an enclave within the larger housing ring. Yet it, too, was completely fortified from the rest of the fort.

The big wigs don't like to rub shoulders with the dirty underlings.

My head shook of its own volition in disgust. It was always the same.

We were floating deep inside the fort, and the third gate further divided one section from another. This was the beginning of the true, true of this fort. People marched in all directions in this area. Most waked with a touch of magic. Unlike the living quarters in the outer ring, where a magic trails was few and far between, here they were everywhere.

The fighters got magic, and the family didn't.

It made sense. Jacques only needed an army, not a family.

Who cares if the next generation has magic?

This generation may never die, so there was no need to think of the future. That was where Jacques had it all wrong.

No one lives forever, not even a Queen.

Maybe the families were not only a buffer but hostages too?

Otherwise, how do you keep your people in line?

Humanity doesn't do well when their loved ones are in peril. They will only fight if they believe it will save them.

Humanity is so predictable.

I could almost weep for them.

George glided over buildings of all shapes and sizes. Most gave off some form of magical wake, alerting me to its contents. All but one, which was a magical dead zone. The exterior waked with the power of iron and a shield. It was the only shield in the entire fort.

The CDC was protected by a great shield, with witches resetting the barrier every time it broke. Yet here, there was only one.

If we land, it will send the entire fort into a tizzy. Dragons do that. I loosed my hunter's vine and stood up. Leaning this way and that, I moved with the motions of George's breathing and wing beats.

The shield was tight to the sides of the building. I guess? Jacques didn't want anyone to know how important this building was. The windows were all sealed tight and blacked out. There was no way to gauge my enemy without entry, and that was what Jacques was counting on.

The roof was vacant. He was confident enough not to order spotters. Cassidy wouldn't have left that empty, no matter how great his shield was.

Stupid Fae, or was he?

My hands moved over my leathers, checking the strapping of knives and the buckles for my sword, crossbow, and long gun. The lump in my pocket reminded me of my rocks. I pulled them out and hummed a trapping spell over them, then shoved them back in my pocket.

I sang a glamor into place and whistled up a mirror. Larka's white hair and light eyes swam before me. She told me enough to trick any human. The glamor would never work on a Fae. But there were only three here, so my odds were good.

This was it. I took a deep breath and slapped both cheeks one after the other. The Jack songs came unbidden with the muscle memory of a lifetime. I sang to be nimble and quick, light as a feather, for the ability to climb any hill, pudding, and pie so I wouldn't run out of energy or become hungry.

Sixpence joined the serenade. I sang every song I could think of and a few more. I sang for the old man to snore, making the rain pour. It would provide cover not only to me but also to Sarah and her people.

"George, I bid you burn this section of the fort to the ground. If I die, you will be free. If I live, I'll free you. Either way, I'm not sure we will meet again."

"You freed me from the Pil's machinations. I will burn and dig until Jacques' corpse lays at my feet. Then I will devour every last drop of him if only to assure myself he is gone and never to return." The chest under my feet rumbled with determination. Good ole George would play his part to the bitter end. Of that, I had no doubt.

"Spoken like a true predator, I wouldn't have it any other way." I snapped my fingers, and the vines disappeared. I took one step and smashed into a portal.

Sarah stepped out to stand next to me. "Where in the fuck do you think you are going?" she demanded. Her wings flared wide, blocking my ability to dart around her. Her bright eyes burned into me as her hand lit up with the same idea. Her wings closed.

"To get Nick," I turned and leaped off the dragon's side. The wind ripped past me faster than I believed it could. The last time I'd embraced a free-fall of this magnitude was the zip in Portland. I sang for light as a feather. The magic barely slowed my descent. I spread my legs and arms along with my hands. The move slowed my downward fall marginally.

A spell wrapped around me. The words were lost to the wind. But my free fall halted, and I drifted down as if I was as light as flotsam and touched down on the roof.

CHAPTER 21

SARAH

Mercia leaped off the dragon into free fall. I almost cried out at her to stop. Yet, my lips slammed closed. We were too close. Any sound would alert the fort.

She was falling so fast. Without a song, she would die. I couldn't let that happen. For Arty's sake, I had to help her.

Selena Gomez and *Slow down* ripped from my mind to my voice box and into the world, carrying the magic to slow Mercia's descent. I didn't want her to stop. However, landing without a splat would be nice.

The magic reached her, wrapping around her appendages and waist. It pulled her back and lowered her as if she was attached to ropes on a crane being lowered into position.

Mercia turned her body to aline with the roof and landed on her feet. She tilted her head back to stare up at me. There was no salute, smile, or thank you.

Not that I expected one.

I blinked, and for a moment, I saw Larka standing there. The visage of Mercia returned. She gave me a crossed arm and walked to the roof door.

I didn't have a plan. Mercia seemed to have one, or so I thought. My heart wanted to jump off and join her to barge into that building and begin killing everything standing in my way.

That was not a plan. That was suicide.

"What did she tell you to do?" I asked George.

"To burn everything to the ground." His big mouth opened, and a blood-curdling roar issued only to turn into a flame. He began circling the fort burning every building on this side of the fence, creating a ring of fire.

I liked George. Fire was practical, keeping people in and out. Reinforcements could only enter if they carried enough magic to live through it. If not, it was one less thief of Fae I had to deal with.

"Carry on, George." I ripped a portal open and stepped through to my Princes and a new attack.

Bonn crossed his left arm over his chest as he lowered his bow, "My Queen." Mod and Wott followed suit, each easing their weapons lower.

"Where is the winter court?"

Mod waved a hand behind her. "The UnSeelie court stands as one," she replied.

Good.

"Send the winter court in first," I shifted on my feet.

"My Queen, why? They have bowed to your demands. There is no reason to kill them off," Mod returned, her face darkened with anger.

"Because I gave them the use of fire, and they can cut a path through the flame wall. For fuck sake, I'm not that vindictive," I growled.

It was insulting. How could she think I would send them to their death just because they didn't bend the knee for me? Some of them I birthed into this fucked up world.

I turned to face the fire, then whirled back around, "They are my children!" I shouted. My hand came to life and radiated heat. I waved it in front of her. "Don't question my dedication to our people. I'm in it to win it. None of us will ever be safe until Jacques is dead."

Mod moved back a step and knelt to the ground with her left arm across her chest and her head lowered.

With my elemental finger, I pushed her chin up to look at me. Her skin crackled like I shoved a white-hot poker into it. Blood cooked on my hand as it wept from the wound. My fire cauterized the injury. I had to pull away. I didn't want to cook her brain too. Even that quick touch was enough to alter her face forever without the possibility of a healing. She whimpered in pain but kept her screams inside.

"I'm first in line on Jacques' death list, and if I'm right, you are right behind me." The coppery scent of cooked blood permeated the air. I hoped it was coming from Mod and not the fort. "So, stop with the bullshit. We don't have the time." My finger was coated in the dry flakes of cooked blood, and I pushed the element away. Once my hand cooled, I rubbed the caked blood on my leather pants.

"Winter cut a path through the flames for your Queen," I shouted over the roar of fire and the dragon. "The rest of you move in with a round if you dare. They know we're here. They will be watching the skies. Jacques thinks he knows all our tricks. So don't give him what he wants."

I could give them all power to wield fire. I could share that. However, I wasn't sure I could claw it back after. There's a reason elementals don't offer that level of control to just anyone.

Aqualis poured onto the ground next to me. "Sarinha," her water voice cooled my rage enough to slow down and listen. She had something to say.

"Terra will not join the fight. She says this battle was always to come, and after the deadfall, their bodies will feed new growth." Then she spit her water on the ground.

I hadn't expected her to join. Rotting corpses are nothing more than compost for a forest. In her mind, death was part of the cycle of life.

"And Aer? Will she partake?" The desire to bite my lip lingered. I couldn't show that kind of weakness to a fellow elemental.

"She may breeze in if a proper opening presents itself. Though I doubt it. She will wait until the fires are all doused before making an appearance. Your fire creates too much turbulence."

"So, it's you and me, kid?" I cracked a half-smile to hide my trepidation.

Fire and water cancel each other out, yet here, we stand shoulder to shoulder.

"My Queen, humanity needs magic to cease its incursions. They will destroy themselves over it. I help you because I see what can happen if I don't. Ignis also saw the dangers. Danu promised she would keep all in check." Aqualis was here for the same reason I was.

"I'm not interested in the promises of a dead person. I swore to end this, no matter what. Even if I wanted to turn away, I couldn't. Magic doesn't take no for an answer."

Aqualis snorted and sprayed water as her laugh grew.

Fuck, that's gross.

Rounds flooded the skies, more than I dreamed would chance iron. Yet Fae had surprised me at every turn.

When I told Winter to cut a path, I forgot to mention the civilians that might get in the way. My wings took flight, and as I reached the first member of the Winter court, I grabbed his wrist before he could cut the woman he held in half.

"Don't kill the innocent, you fool." I backhanded him, and his body twisted before falling to the ground. I moved my focus to the woman, "Get your family and leave while you still can. The Government is using fairy blood to build an army, and we are here to stop them."

Her face was covered in soot and fear. Tears streaked her cheeks. She grabbed her two children, beckoned to another, and ran toward the forest.

"Call for the protection of Terra. She will shield you!" I yelled. The woman never even glanced behind her to make sure the older child kept pace. I opened a portal to the far side of the winter court just before the flaming wall.

I hummed, *We will rock you*, by Queen to elevate my voice, "Do not kill the innocent!" I growled. "You would make us no better than them. Anyone without Fae blood and not lifting a weapon for attack, let them go." Most of the winter court bypassed whatever human was in their way. A few kicked them before letting them go.

But no one else died, and that was all I wanted. In some way, we had to come out of this righteous, if not clean. In my heart, I knew humanity did this.

They always take what isn't theirs like a four-year-old. They snatch it away and scream mine, then refuse to give it back.

Humanity found a way to have magic. Like anyone who steals something precious, they will kill to keep it.

Rocks rose in the air around me at the thought. The ground shook, and buildings cracked. The siding buckled and puckered while the sound of glass cracking and shattering reached me. I couldn't pull my anger back. The power of fire burned within me, the heat filtering out to the tips of my toes. I still didn't understand how to control it.

"My Queen, think of the forest. The green of the trees. The peace that can only come from the cool air and the freedom to run," Bonn soothed.

I turned to see his face. It was filled with understanding.

Control. I need control.

The vision he'd whispered was calming. The taste of moss in the air eased the need to burn.

"Focus on the houses around us. If you call to the minerals in the structures, you can pull them down," he added.

I didn't want to pull them down. This was base housing. Everyone living here was family to a serviceman of some kind. I was once one of them, with no idea what went on in the base. I was just a kid.

Guilt flooded my system. There were kids here everywhere, and we were destroying their lives.

"No, we aren't here for the civilians. Just Janice and Jacques," I replied.

My rapidly beating wings stilled at my back. The grass in front of every house was dead from the cold, not fire. When we left, the people here may die. It pricked at me because we would be the cause.

I could fix it later.

I'll just add it to my list of things to do.

"Move forward! Leave as much intact on this side of the fire as possible." My orders were to be obeyed. Fae didn't defy a Queen without understanding the consequences.

My flying rocks whipped around me, creating a tornado of protection. As I approached the wall of fire. My hand illuminated the outer skin blacken and cracked, leaving trace lines of glowing lave underneath. I raised my spread fingers, and the wall of flame parted like the Red Sea for Moses. The ground smoked, and I moved forward. The soil under my feet should have been hot, though I couldn't feel it. Instead, I felt nothing at all. The power of fire shielded me from all of it.

Fae from all courts dashed around me and rushed to the fight on the other side. My parted fire gave me tunnel vision into the chaos on the flipside. Men ran and screamed in every direction. All waked with the power of magic and tasted of changeling.

None carried pure blood. They all bled red, not a single one blue.

I breached the opening and joined the fray, slashing the first body that came my way. I didn't stay to watch the Quicksilver march of death. Instead, I moved on to the next thief and cut him down too.

My rocks slammed into the enemies' bodies and pummeled them to the ground until they stopped moving. I hadn't bothered to sing. I didn't want to kill an innocent on accident. I didn't want to be THEM.

A bullet pushed into the palm of my left hand and out the other side. The pain shot up my arm, and I screamed. Lava flowed into the wound, sealing the hole and healing it completely.

A second bullet hit my shoulder. I stumbled back and bit my lip, then hummed for a protection shield. My lava blood healed that hole too.

Am I lucky? Or am I just walking the line of what the fuck?

The man on the roof disappeared, as did his shots. I moved forward. Mercia must have killed him. Perhaps he died. It didn't matter. Janice was here somewhere, and I wasn't waiting for someone to point the way. The buildings were standard military build before the Govs turned it over to subdivisions.

All the lights that weren't broken were on. Fae can see in the dark. These blood thieves would, too, though not as well as a real Fae.

My wings pushed down, and I rose into the sky. Bullets flew in every direction, and I batted the iron missiles away.

When I was high enough in the air, I surveyed the area, looking for a power source.

CHAPTER 22

MERCIA

The shield burned, and my feet wanted to find another way off the roof. There was no way I would go back. Nick was here somewhere. I was going to fight my way to wherever he was.

A small tower of a door perched on the roof, cutting a divide between it and the dark sky. Hunched down on one side of the roof was a snipper. His weapon was covered in a dark fabric to hide the barrel and the scope.

He was like me. He hunted alone. Most humans moved in pairs. The wakes coming off his body spoke of a bit of magic. For him, it was enough.

My feet barely touched the roof as I moved across the black tar paper. Each step burned with the tight shield that covered everything. The man hardly moved as he slid the bolt to release his casing. The ting of metal hitting the ground on top of metal was the only sound I heard over the roar of battle that raged all around us. He pushed a fresh round into place and waited for a moment, then squeezed the trigger.

He was a pro. His every move was orderly and in complete control. His breath was even and measured. He pulled his eye away from the scope and tilted his head to one side as if to listen.

I flashed to his side and pressed my dagger to his neck. This was a clever killer, a man with skills like my own.

He should know something.

"Where are the Fae?" I asked. His breathing didn't change, and his heart rate didn't pick up.

Oh, this will be fun.

"Jacques," he said. "Keeps them out of sight." He offered up too easily.

He rolled over, knocking the blade from my hand, kicking me in the chin. I stumbled back and hummed a shield, then added *come back, Peter,* to retrieve the blade.

He kipped up and charged me. I sidestepped, and tripped him. The hunter's vine song was second nature to me. The vines sprout from the ground, twining around his legs. Yet, he whistled a cutting tune.

My lips peeled back in a smile.

I could finish him quickly and move on.

Instead, I decided to toy with him. I needed information. I flashed behind him and slashed at his back. He groaned a tune to protect the injury. In a heartbeat, I flashed to the front, leaving a fresh cut on his chest.

Before I could flash away, his hand was around my neck. I laughed as he squeezed to close my airway. He whistled to hold me still. However, my vine would never stop.

Not as long as I'm alive.

It twisted around his torso and up his chest to tighten on his neck. He stopped whistling, and the spell was released. I pried his hand away from my neck and pressed my blade into his. A little blood peeked out from the skin at the tip. "How do you know?" I growled. I hummed a bit of the hunter's curse as the rivulet from his neck hit my skin. It was enough to drain some of his strength.

He swallowed. The weakness that came from my hunter's curse must have hit him. He knew I had him by the balls. With the vine curled around him, I pull the rifle free of his body and toss it over the side.

He's not going to need that anymore.

"I saw them. Once." His breath was coming quick as my vines tightened around his chest, compressing his lungs.

Can't sing if you can't breathe. Rule number one.

Sarah taught me that.

"Great, where?" I hissed.

A moment later, the flap of wings just over our heads broke the bubble of interrogation. It was George. He was raining a fresh round of fire on the humans below. The scent of cooking flesh reached me, and I wanted to gag.

"Is your family down there somewhere? Maybe I should go look for them after you and I are done?" I asked, looking over the side of the building. I was not going to hurt them, yet the threat was implied.

"Jacques isn't here, not in this building. Neither are those Fae fucks he took—" I slapped the side of his head.

"Are they still alive?" I asked. My outer demeanor was calm. Maintaining that illusion grew harder by the moment.

I'm eager. Too eager.

I couldn't help it. Nick was close by. I could taste it. His magic called to me, just out of reach.

"Jacques had them near the plant, I think. Please don't hurt my family," he pleaded.

Yuck, maybe I was wrong. He's not like me at all. I wouldn't beg. I'd spit in his face and rail. His family was safe from me, *as long as they're still human, of course.*

"Did your family steal Fae blood, like you?" I dug the knife at his throat just a little more.

"No, they didn't get the bone marrow transplant. Only the fighters did," he replied. The trauma of me cutting into him changed his wakes. They grew stronger, and now I could see the color of his magic. It was moss green.

The same as Nick's.

"Who's marrow did you get?" I screamed at him and dug the knife in as I shook his body.

The virus of fear spread like wildfire from my chest to every inch of my body. I pulled my knife away from his neck and slapped one side of his face and then the other.

"Tell me!" I shrieked. As my body shook with rage.

"The younger one. I don't know his name. Jacques called him the bastar—" his voice cut out just as my blade cut the box it came from.

It was Nick. He took Nick's blood. The feeling in my belly boiled as a fresh round of the poison fear pumped into my flesh.

I sang for the Fae fire to burn him to the ground, then stood up and stared at the sky.

Should I believe him when he said Nick wasn't here?

The interior of the building was filled with pitfalls and locked rooms. Of that, I was sure. But a power plant… that would be well guarded. Any power generation plant after the fall was worth more than gold. You could live like a king with that.

Any Warlock worth a shit would be there.

I snapped my fingers. Overhead, George locked his maw shut, cutting off the flames spewing over another building. His great wings raised and lowered as he lifted and turned to thumped down on the roof. "Master."

"I need a ride."

He lowered a shoulder and stretched out his leg, and I climbed aboard.

CHAPTER 23

SARAH

Wherever the power source was, it had to be on the base. This entire fort was designed for nuclear fallout. It would be close. A microsystem that was able to continue long after the rest of the grid was gone.

Water.

Rivers don't change course often. Their flows remain much the same. I was looking for a dam or hydro plant of some kind.

That idea was quelched. There were no rivers nearby. The scent of salt lingered in the air more than that of freshwater or the minerals of a spring.

I circled the fort. There was a building set away from the others that gave off more heat than was necessary. That had to be the source.

Now to figure out what they are using to power it.

I dove to the ground and cracked open a portal to stand next to the building. The stench of bio-mass hit me like a wall. This was just another barter town methane plant. To reiterate what I already knew, the sound of snorting followed the stench.

It was a good plan to keep pigs to make methane as well as a meat source. They provide gas to turn the genny and food for the table. They only needed enough power for the fort.

I had to be honest. This place was a small town run by the US Government.

How did Jacques fit in?

My natural instinct for self-preservation kicked in, and I hummed a glamor. They would see the me before the Queen's search. The fake human me. The old me.

If I thought about it too long, the glamor would fail. So, the feelings that came with my glamor got poured into a bottle and set on the self of shit I couldn't think about ever. Janice needed me too much for a big cry fest.

I sang songs from my childhood to lighten my feet and quicken my steps. I added some strength to the brew and moved forward to the nearest door.

A steel door was standard issue commercial construction with a matching steel frame. The lock was not. Besides the wakes of a spell song dancing around the frame, a magnetic field sang to me also. I searched this side of the building for another door. There was one, and it too had the same problem.

Breaking this lock wasn't going to be quiet. I pulled the shadows to me and tip-toed around the side of this building. Across a narrow driveway was another set of buildings. The major heat production was coming from there.

That should be the generators.

Before the Queen's search, I read about Tesla. He invented the generator with Westinghouse as his investor. Westinghouse screwed Tesla out of any profits, of course. But Westinghouse still made the best gennies for mass power production. I was ready to bet that was what was running in there. Those machines would be decades old, running on parts just as old or older.

Machines don't like metal shavings. They like fresh good parts.

The spell blocking the other doors lingered here too. I moved the end of the building with the exhaust stacks. That room would have the most noise. Gennies aren't quiet. Power generation is a noisy, smelly business.

The song locking the door worked twofold. It locked and alerted.

The moment I break the spell, this place will blare alarms to kingdom come.

So, I worked the maglock off first.

An old Rave song called Set me Free by Planet Soul came to mind, and the magic did the trick.

The wakes of the spells lining the door were silver, like Jacques. He sang this spell himself. The longer I looked at it, the more apparent it became that Jacques didn't understand the human world at all.

His song waked over the door and the portion of the frame the door sat in. The wall around the frame carried no trace of the song.

When something is in your way, you get rid of it.

Wolfshiem - I Find You're Gone was all it took for the door and frame to vanish, leaving the frame out from the builder. On the other side was a clean room with not a soul in sight.

Jacques was a little too confident. I changed my glamor. The human Sarah's face was fine for walking about, but Jacques saw me when I was still human. Zoe's face came to me readily, and I clothed myself with her visage. No one alive would remember her other than me.

I added a uniform similar to the CDC's security personnel.

That should be enough to throw anyone not fully Fae off.

I walked in like a boss/queen.

The purr of the gennies filled every nook and cranny with a controlled hum. Off to the larger side of the room, pipes snaked away from the enormous machines. Before anyone spotted me, I used my power over rock, minerals, and fire to pull every particle I could from the surrounding area. The minuscule pieces of rock came through the door to hover at my beck and call.

My left hand glowed with a tight-fisted elemental control. When I opened my hand, the sandy granules engulfed the machines clogging every orifice. They sputtered, the lights flickered, and a slow high, pitched grinding replaced the purr.

The first genny on the line ground to a halt and began to heat up. The power of song-filled me, and the disco version of Brick House came to mind. I smashed the side of the machine. The giant turbine flew out of the casing and smashed into a wall, embedding itself in the concrete. The flanges glowed with the power of fire. Part of the first machine must have hit the second because a screeching came just before the casing burst outward and a flywheel spun across the room at a hundred miles an hour.

My fingers closed, and fire closed in on the final three units, heating the partials to a thousand degrees Kelvin. Elemental power waked out from the source, melting the metal struts in the walls and ceiling. The roof creaked and sagged.

A moment later, a door slammed open.

The silver-eyed asshole calmly stepped through. A wiry smile scraped across his face. Jacques took me in from head to toe. He took a deep breath.

"My beautiful Queen wife."

What the actual fuck?

CHAPTER 24

MERCIA

We circled the enclave, searching for the plant. I didn't know what I was looking for. My CB in Portland derived all its power from a hydro plant on the river. We used water for micro-hydro plants all over the roof systems, collecting water and directing it into the units. It rained a lot in Portland.

This wasn't water power. Texas used a lot of solar. This was different. One thing I did know was that power creates heat.

Just then, George turned for another round, and an explosion rocked a building well away from the rest of the complex.

Bingo!

Sarah was probably doing what she does best - tearing shit down.

I smiled. If Sarah was a wreaking ball that dropped a building on your head, I was the invisible poison you took in without being aware it would kill you. A second blast joined the first, and George winged his way toward the glowing building with a sagging roofline.

"Do you want me to land, master?"

"Naw, go burn some shit."

"Is Jacques in there?"

"Maybe, I don't know, but I think Nick is and that's my target. Go find your own!"

George flew low over the structure and slid off his back. The lyrics of Sarah's song came back to me, and I slowed my descent, landing by a hole in the burning building just in time to spot Jacques' leering smile.

"My beautiful Queen wife."

Yuck! Why are all Fae males so gross?

They all acted like sex was always the first thing on their mind. Jacques may have been pretty— pretty doesn't make up for ants crawling over your skin creepy. I'd seen enough warlocks that acted the same way.

No, thank you! I'm good.

I pulled my hunter cloak tight and slithered into the building, hugging walls. I would just flitter across the room to find out what was in room number two. A few Fae thieves filtered out behind Jacques, blocking the access to the space beyond.

Pixie shit!

Sarah came alone.

What for?

She had enough people to overrun this area three times over.

Why leave the bulk of her army?

I didn't want to wait and find out the answer. Instead, I headed out the way I came and flashed around to the other side of the building and the main doors.

A squad of fake Fae guarded the main doors. I dipped back around a corner, slapped either cheek and then called for Jacques to make me quick and nimble. I needed to get into the house that Jack built. A glamor of the sniper from the roof settled over me, bringing an itch I couldn't get rid of. His jacket carried his name.

Hicks.

I would be fine as long as no one asked my first name.

I rounded the corner, keeping to the shadows until I was right next to the first guard. "I was told to move to the roof," I announced.

The entire squad jumped out of their skin. The normal human reaction is fear. Its taste flavored the air, and the sticky candy goodness hit me full force. Their weapons were all trained on me, "Whoa! Lieutenant Hicks reporting. Put me on the roof," I said, injecting as much fear as I dared into my voice. I held up a paper with fake orders.

The Capitan grabbed the paper and didn't give it a glance. He gave me the once over and tilted his head at the door. "The stairs are inside. There's a ladder to the roof. There's no cover up there."

"Understood." I tilted my head at him in a salute.

The men stepped aside, and I pushed the door in. The lights flickered and went out. I took the opportunity and pulled my shadowy cloak. Most of the doors waked with a magic spell, each the color of silver.

Momma said Jacques was silver in magic and eye color. She told me if I ever met him to run. She didn't believe I would survive. The UnSeelie didn't like changelings.

That's okay.

I didn't like them either. The pull of the courts didn't work on me.

The hallway led closer to the burning room's heat where Sarah and Jacques were. I didn't need to join that party. Nick was here somewhere. My hunter sense told me he was close. A man rushed down the hall for the plant room, and I flattened into a doorway.

As the man moved, the scent of a wolf drifted behind him. The color of his magic waked the moss green of Nick. I whipped my head around to follow him out the door at the far end. The hunter in me wanted to give chase, to kill. But that wasn't my objective. I turned my eyes back the way the man came, and the pull of my love was all it took. Like honey to a bee, I let my heart follow the magic wake line back to its origin.

It took me upstairs and right to a door that waked with Jacques' magic. Without a thought, I slammed my foot into the door. It didn't budge. The magic holding it closed was too great, and I couldn't undo the song holding it closed. There's always another way. I looked up and around. The walls waked of cement and of reinforced concrete. The inner walls were crossed with rebar. The trace amounts of iron created a grid of protection.

But every building had heat and needed air movement. Humanity puts great stock in fresh air. Not two steps away was an intake cover. I hooked the tip of my crossbow into the louvers and pulled the thing down, then tossed it away.

Magic loves to help when you ask, and the Jack songs made me light as a feather, so I jumped into the duct with grace and stealth. I called for *come back, Peter* and the grate closed behind me.

No need to inform them of where to look if they come looking.

I shimmied to the first junction and turned left. I worked my way over to the room where that fake Fae exited and peered down into the space. The room carried three bodies, all hooked up to IVs, sleeping the sleep of the might as well be dead, and two guards.

That kind of living death wasn't to my taste.

I'd rather be dead.

Nick wasn't one of them, but a black hair full Fae was. He carried the look of a warrior. With or without Nick, I could use that guy. He would help me. One of the other beds had a female changeling. She wasn't far from being full Fae. Her hair was blond with black tips. Her belly was full with a baby. She looked like she'd been there a while too. Her muscles didn't carry the vigor of movement.

The life inside her moved like an eel just under the surface. There was no reason to free her. She was close to her time, and I didn't need a changeling going into labor in the middle of a fight. She would have to stay. The other body was a woman who looked much like the first with blond/black hair. She was strong, a changeling in her prime.

In a low voice, I sang:

"Little Miss Muffet sat on a tuffet, filling with drugs and whey; Along came a spider." Three little black spiders with red stars on their bellies slipped down from the duct cover.

They landed on the beds. "*Who sat down beside her, And cut the drugs away.*" Each spider chewed the little tube pumping *Danu knows what into these Fae.*

I tried to decide if fighting was a good use of my time or not. Stealth was still the top priority for me to find Nick. The guards hadn't noticed the spiders or the drugs running out of the little hoses yet, but one would before too long. So, I sang, "*it's raining, it's pouring, the old man is snoring.*"

I kicked the grate out and slipped into the room. The first guard attempted to take to his feet. A crossbow bolt was planted in his chest, and he fell to the floor not far from the door. The second was already slumped on the floor. He waked of Fae magic. But it was not his own. I pulled a dagger and plunged it into his heart. The moss green coloring faded away with his life.

"That's for taking what belongs to another," I murmured like a lover in his ear.

I moved to the Fae warrior first and slapped either cheek and sang for sixpence to wake him. His eyes drowsed open and rolled around in his head.

I cupped his chin and turned his face this way and that. He was beautiful in the male Fae way. His magic waked of violets and lilacs. I slapped him again, and his eyes opened. The amethyst orbs widened at me.

"Sarah," he whispered. His leg on one side was bandaged. I pulled the dressing back to inspect the patch job. There were human stitches all neatly in a row.

Well, well, Janice. This must be my lucky day, a warrior and a tactician all in one.

It had to be. I sang for sixpence again and slapped the Wyld out of him. He sat up and held both my wrists away from his face. "Where is Sarinha?" He demanded. "Who are you?" then winced, his hand flying to his hip.

"Who's and where's will have to wait. You need to get up and help me find Nick!" I ordered. He released my arms, and I sang every Jack song in my mental library. Sixpence twice.

He stood up and stared me down, "You are Pil's child, by Arthur," he stated while favoring the injured hip.

I rolled my eyes, "Yeah. Anyway, we have to move."

I climbed on the bed of the changeling and began my wake-up combo again. I had to sing for sixpence four times and slap her so hard her cheek bruised. Finally, her eyes fluttered open, and she gasped as she sat up. She never looked at me but the woman in the bed next to her.

"We have to wake her," she said and attempted to turn over. I had her pinned to the bed with my body weight.

"No way. She's ready to burst. We are in the middle of a battle. I need fighters not gestating changelings with the muscle tone of a jellyfish," I replied.

"I will not leave my sister here to die," the woman retorted.

Her gaze traveled over Janice and widened in recognition. The plants in the room began growing at an alarming rate. She tried to scuttle away, her legs working to push off the bed.

"Whoa, back off, green thumb! I'm here to get my boyfriend, Nick, and if you or your gestating sister get in my way, I'm going to lock you up with a song and leave you behind. Got it?" I growled at her, then moved between her and the sleeping baby machine.

"Nick?" she asked, "Nick, dark hair and green eyes, friends with Sarah?" The changeling asked. She was already off the bed with her back against the wall, inching toward the door.

"We don't have time for question and answer. Leave your sister. I will glamor her and shield her. The potion will run out, and she will wake on her own. The shield will release her. By then, the battle will be decided," Janice broke in. He looked from me to the woman and back.

"That works for me," I replied and turned to leave. I didn't want to answer the woman. She'd said Nick's name with awe. That grated on my nerves. I didn't need a warlock lover getting in my way.

Nick is mine, and I don't share.

"Is Sarah here too?" She asked.

I gave her a side glance, "Yeah, she's downstairs, having a tete with her husband," I remarked and then immediately wished I'd kept my mouth shut.

Janice pulled a dagger from my leathers and disappeared out the door.

Pixie shit! Why can't I keep my mouth shut? Now, my warrior is gone.

The woman glanced down at the floor and back up at me. The sorry I thought would come didn't. Instead, she said,

"Curiosity killed the cat. I'll help you find Nick. After all, he saved my life."

I stopped dead halfway down the hall. "When?"

"He and Sarah went into the Hallowed Hills and freed me after that Fae, Janice, stole me away." She hooked her thumb in the direction Janice went.

Ugh!

The circles within circles of the Fae world left me dizzy. All I wanted was Nick.

"What's your name?" I asked, even though I was probably going to forget in a few minutes if she died.

"Olive."

Typical. It was an earthy name, and she grew plants. Probably offspring from the spring court.

It figures.

I moved to the next door, no longer caring about stealth. I sang for the London bridge to fall down, and the wall shook.

"Don't overdo it. The building will come down," the changeling chided. She placed her hand on the wall and hummed for a moment. Ropey vines worked their way out of the cracks and pulled the cement apart.

I joined her and sang for my hunter's vine. The wall contorted, and great chunks of cement held by vines pulled away, creating a hole. Inside sat three guys, each pointing a gun at the wolf chained to the floor with iron.

Nick!

CHAPTER 25

SARAH

Jacques saw through my glamor.

They don't work on the full-bloods.

I really wish they did. He smirked at me, and stepped deeper into the room and closer to the fire. My hand ached with the power held at bay.

I wasn't going to hold it for long. Rather than wait for him to get closer, I tossed a flaming ball at him. It never hit its mark. The flame sputtered and disappeared.

"Awe, Sarinha, how charming. You wish to kill me. Perhaps Janice didn't tell you enough. The Queen can't kill the King and vice versa." He rubbed his hands together. When he pulled them apart, the center was a sticky mess of spider webs. He smashed his hands together again, creating more. He strung them out, letting them droop between each hand.

My mouth went dry.

"Is that why you never wanted to be King?" I asked to take my mind off the webbed stick mass growing between his hands.

"It's so much easier to kill when magic doesn't get in the way. Don't you think?" He cocked a brow at me while his hands worked on the sticky mass that was forming.

I hummed some Huey Lewis and The News - Back in time, hoping it would bring my army to bear on this site.

"Is that what the red stone was for, to begin with?"

I pushed the flames out of the room. There was no need to destroy the building. The power was already out, and the emergency lights were on. The power was never coming back.

"The red stone?" He laughed, "The King didn't kill the Queen with it. He drained her dry."

"No shit, Sherlock! But why?" I hummed Queen - Who wants to live forever. Yet, the magic never took hold. I was powerless, and Jack just kept mushing his web.

"I'm not going to kill you, you know," he replied. His clothes were medieval in nature. The long black robes of a mage or wizard edged with black fur to set off his hair. Lending the silver look more of a stark contrast.

"Yeah? What are you going to do?" I asked as the quivering of my insides took hold.

"I shall not kill you, like your beloved Janice," he laughed.

I screamed, and the walls shook with my anger. "It's raining, it's pouring, the old man is snorting." In the distance, over everything, someone else was singing the same song. I renewed my efforts. "He went to bed,"

The ceiling contorted and tore open to reveal the heavy cloud-filled sky. Big fat drops of rain fell on my head. What was left of my fire never went out. "And bumped his head." A beam crashed down, barely missing Jacques's head. "And couldn't get up in the morning—"

Janice crashed through the doorway and right into Jacques, knocking him to the ground. They rolled across the floor, grappling with each other for the upper hand.

The magic may not let me kill him, but I can help someone else get the job done.

Three henchmen by the door moved in, singing Jack songs.

Pathetic.

I hummed a shield over all of them and watched as they pounded at the barrier. All three carried a violet wake line.

My eyes darted to Janice. His hip was bleeding.

I sang for *a lime in the coconut,* and fifty coconuts dropped from the sky, each crashing into Jacques. The healing song came quick and dirty from my lips, and Janice roared in pain. However, I cut the song short, giving him all the strength he needed to continue.

"Sarah!" He yelled and moved to join me.

"Don't worry about me. Fight! I can't use magic to kill him. He's my King!" I shouted and pulled my Quicksilver, then tossed it at him.

He grabbed it from the sky with a knowing hand and slashed it at Jacques' looming form. I did what I did best. I pulled a rabbit out of a hat. I joined in the fray. The finger daggers on my bodice came free with an ease I'd didn't think I had. I tossed the first one at Jacques, and it ripped through his side and veered away.

The second never made it as Jacques whistled to block the weapon. Magic was helping him.

Fuck! Time to change tactics.

With every tossed, I aimed to harm, not kill.

If magic doesn't let me lay a killing blow, then death by a thousand cut it shall be.

I called the daggers back to my hand and began again. I tossed them as if it was a carnival show, and I merely wanted to pierce him to the ground. Janice slashed with Silver and stabbed with a dagger one after the other. Jacques dodged and leaped as if this was a show in New York at the Met, and there was no danger at all.

Nursery rhythms like I'd never heard came and went, as did the magic that did or did not take. Janice was powerful and quick. He managed to stab Jacques several times. But Jacques sang a song to stitch the wounds closed. It stemmed the blood flow, but that was about it.

The building shook, and a crash came from somewhere close by, yet out of sight. I tossed and recalled my blades over and over. This wasn't getting me any closer to killing Jacques, and kill him I would. It was the only way.

My gun hung under my arm. It was an old friend from my life before. The only change was the iron-tipped bullets. I couldn't touch them. The poison would infect me as surely as black death from a flea. Jacques had to know about guns by now and how they worked. With Janice distracting him, perhaps I could finish this once and for all.

Magic may not let me kill him, but guns kill people every day.

I squeezed the trigger without taking aim. Cernunnos tried to sing the sure-shot song over my weapon, but where was the fun in that? I liked the thrill of a free shot. The bullet missed by a few inches. Jacques' eyes met mine.

"Wife?" He called.

"Don't fucking call me that, you heartless puke!" I yelled and took fresh aim. Yet, this shot missed too. After that, I just rained what was left all over him. Only waiting to miss Janice.

Janice's shield should keep them out should.

The bullets never landed, not one, and the trigger's clicking told me I was out. A moment later, a blast of magic hit me full force, knocking me back to a wall. Jacques had a dagger shoved in Janice's chest and Silver in his left hand. When my eyes stopped rolling around in my head, I took in the scene.

Jacques planned this.

God, I hate him.

I tried to pull away from the wall, but I was stuck. My head lolled around, and my eyes landed on my impediment. Webbing held me fast against the wall.

Jacques flashed to my side. His hand cupped my cheek, and he whispered sung, *"A wise old owl lived in an oak. The more he saw, the less he spoke. The less he spoke, the more he heard. Why can't we all be like that wise old bird?"* A slow lazy smile worked its way over his face. He leaned in and placed a soft kiss on my lips.

My throat worked, but no sound issued forth. I coughed on the smoke in the air and tried again. Nothing. My screams were locked inside, and the release I desperately needed didn't come. My breath came in huffs. Hysteria was just on the edge of my psyche. I looked at Janice. His chest lifted and lowered, the blade shifting with each breath. If Jacques pulled the blade out, he'd bled out and die.

My hand erupted in flame, burning the webbing away. Before Jacques could stop me, I flashed to Janice's side and gripped the blade with my fiery hand, heating it up and burning the wound from the inside out. Janice wailed in agony.

The building shook as a section of wall grew vines and flowers. The honeysuckle trickled in and grew to separate the cracks before bursting into blooms and perfuming the air. Then the wall crumbled away, leaving an opening.

A moment later, Jacques' fist collided with the side of my head. The only thing I could see was Mercia and stars.

CHAPTER 26

MERCIA

Olive squeaked and jumped back. "Where's Nick?" She demanded. The three men didn't react quite as nicely.

"Come any closer—"

"And you'll kill him?" I asked with a cocked eyebrow. "Or you'll shoot me? Same old, same old. How about I counter your threat with a few of my own. You know who I am, right?" I looked at each of them in turn. One gulped.

Good.

"Put down your weapons, and I'll only pull the Fae from you. Don't, and I'll kill each of you." I smiled. This was going to be fun. A challenge.

Olive didn't see what I saw. "Nick isn't here. Let's leave them to their dog."

"Nick is the dog, you twit." I never let the smile leave my lips. Olive gasped.

"Jacques will kill us," the first man stated.

Good, we had a leader. Kill him first.

"Jacques will kill you anyway," I countered and hummed for the lock around Nick's neck to release. It didn't give.

Next plan.

Olive didn't wait for me to make my move. Instead, she pulled flowers from the walls and whipped the vines around their guns. I was caught off guard. I didn't usually work with a pal. I pulled the trigger on my bow and shot the first guy in the eye. He fell dead, only to be caught by a vine and held upright.

Olive flashed to the next guy, dug her fingers into his eye-sockets, and smiled as he screamed.

I stabbed the third one, but he got a song off before his life was over. It hit Olive full force and slammed her against the wall, knocking all the air from her lungs.

She cried in pain as a piece of metal protruded from her abdomen. "Don't stop! Save my sister, Zoe," she coughed.

The vines curled back and pulled away. The blind man screamed on the floor, groping for anything.

Nick whined.

I grabbed the guy's arm and drug him over to Olive. "Fae don't die. We find a way to fight on," I calmly replied. I pulled her away from the wall. Bluish blood poured from the front hole. I was sure there was as much coming from the back. The man swung his arm as if to punch me. I moved a fraction of an inch, then slammed my fist into his head. He slumped to the floor.

"This is going to hurt," I supplied.

The man groaned before I cut his chest open and thrust my hand into his chest cavity. Agony filled the room from my victim and Olive. My right hand channeled the life from one to the other. Her chest wound worked its way closed, and the blood flow ceased.

Olive lay on her side, crying. I pulled my bloody hand out and whipped it on the dead guy's chest, then began searching bodies for keys.

Nick whined and nudged the guy I shot in the eye. I moved to that body and in the front right pocket was a ring of keys. I ripped the pocket open and snatched the keys.

The locks were all iron and burned with every touch. I ripped some fabric from a shirt and used it as a potholder to hold the locks as I tried the keys. None of them worked.

"Fucccck!"

I moved to the second guy and repeated the process. Nothing. He didn't have even one key. My blood rider, on the other hand, had keys in every pocket. "What's the deal with you? Hum?" I inquired of the corpse. I ripped and pulled until the pile of keys lay on the ground, slightly wet with blood but none the worse for wear.

I didn't need to try most of them because they were labeled as *master key*. Part of my thought it was funny. I kept that inside. Nick whimpered and nudged both of his back legs. The hidden laugh evaporated.

Both Nick's legs were poorly bandaged and limp on the ground. "I'm working on it, baby. Don't worry." My fingers burned from the iron of the locks, and none of the keys were working.

"You need to try the black one," Olive offered.

I growled at her, and the shiver of the change began its work. Nick yipped. I glanced at him. "Don't worry, I got it," I muttered. The change came to a halt, and I mentally pushed it back. The black key sizzled against my skin, and I sucked in air to keep my cries behind my teeth. My fabric pot holder only kept the lion's share of the heat at bay. The key slid into the lock and snicked. I sighed.

Nick's neck was free. I released his legs, and the change worked over him until his human form lay in a heap before me naked. He shivered, and goosebumps rose over his body.

"Mercia," he coughed. His legs were covered in wounds. They used him like a mine and kept digging at every fresh patch.

"Don't. Save your strength. The pain isn't over yet."

"No, I don't have it in me. Just go help Sarah. You can heal me later." He pushed me to leave. There was no force behind it. He was too weak to fight. His skin color and his wakes told me if I left him here, he wouldn't live the day out. Jacques must have been doing something to keep him alive. It wasn't enough. Or that was exactly what he wanted, just enough and not too much.

Those human tears I couldn't get away from rushed forward. "No. I won't leave you. Not again. NO!" The pain in my chest tore at me. "I swear by all that I am to Danu and Puca, I will never leave you. Ever. I never should have left before," a deep growl followed.

His hand cupped my cheek. I leaned in and kissed him. "I love you," I murmured.

"I know." He quirked a half-smile and winked at me.

A throat cleared, "Use me." Olive said, her hands clasped in front of her.

"Use you for what?" I asked without looking at her.

Nick refocused on Olive, "Olive? You're so young and Fae." he marveled.

"Yes, hi." She waved, her black and blonde hair hanging limp with blood here and there.

"No, we can't use her," he started to yell and groaned with the pain while holding his belly.

"Yes, you can. Zoe told me how you and Sarah went to save me. I wouldn't be here without you. Just promise that you will help Zoe and her baby." She tipped her chin up as her jaw quivered in fear. The wakes around her lost that floral kaleidoscope and turned a sour yellow.

She was offering to let me kill her for Nick. I glanced at Nick and back at Olive. I'd never met anyone willing to give their life for another.

"I don't have to kill, you know. It would just be enough so he could survive a healing song."

"Really? Well, then, what are you waiting for?" She burst with joy and relief.

"I thought the hunter's curse killed," Nick murmured.

I shook my head. "I can use it just for a top-up or weaken my prey. I don't have to take it all. A siphon from another changeling, you need even less. Human blood doesn't give you much life force."

Olive laid down next to Nick and lifted her shirt, exposing her belly.

I lowered her shirt and shook my head. "I don't need to cut your belly open. A cut on your wrist will do. I'm not taking that much." I lifted her arm and sliced across her tiny wrist. She was really a tiny fairy doll. She hissed at the pain, and I wrapped my hand around her wrist and squeezed.

"Ouch."

I ignored her cries and laid my other hand on Nick's chest over his heart. The magic of Fae coursed through me, and it was wowy zowy. I'd never tasted anything like it. I'd never ridden the blood of a Fae or a changeling. This was the sweet drug Momma spoke about. I'd always believed ridding the blood of a human was the same. This was sooo much different. I could taste their magic on both sides. Nick's was like his scent, Redbull and Axe cologne. While Olive was the flower garden at Puca's cottage. Every flower all at once.

The witches in New Orleans were nothing more than a flavor of Fae. This was a drink for the ages.

"Mercia," Nick called. "Mercia!"

I came back from the ride, and Olive was crying. I released her arm and leaned away.

"I took too much," I replied. It wasn't a *sorry*.

I wasn't.

She sniffled and pulled her arm to her, cradling the wrist to her breast. "It's okay. It was for Nick."

The wolf inside me growled low.

"She knows I'm yours, and you are mine. Don't kill her," Nick soothed, petting me.

I wiped the blood on one of the dead guys, knelt before Nick, and sang the healing song. Nick moaned and screamed. The healing went on for what seemed forever, but it was only a moment. He lay on the floor, sweating in pain. I sang some of the clothes from the dead guy with the head wound, then wrapped Nick in them.

The building shook before the screeching of metal being ripped apart filled the air.

"Come on, baby. Sarah needs us. You need to get up. I need you too." I smacked his cheek, just enough to get his eyes open.

"I'll be fine. Float me next to you."

"No way, I need Nick the fighter, not Nick the pincushion." I sang for sixpence three times, and he was on his feet. After that, I added all the Jack crack I could throw into the mix along with a few others.

"Sing, come back, Peter, for your sword," I instructed.

He sang the words, but the sword didn't show up. "It's probably still in New Orleans," he offered and shrugged.

"Then grab a gun." I ran my hand over his shoulders to assure myself he was in fighting order.

I stopped to look up into his moss-green eyes. He pulled me by my neck to him and kissed me like a hungry man. I gave as good as I got.

"I knew you loved me," he smirked.

I smacked his arm and turned on a heel, heading out the door. Rather than take the stairs, I walked to the end of the hallway with the shared wall to the generator room.

"Olive, help me bring this wall down."

"Sure thing." She sang for sunflowers and edelweiss, honeysuckle, rosemary, and sage. They were all songs I didn't know, yet each one brought a new scent and strong ropey branches into the cracks of the cement. I added my hunter's vine, and we ripped a hole in the wall. The smoky air bursts into the hallway like a cloud moves in the sky. I coughed and stared down into the smoky room. Janice lay with my knife blade buried in his chest, and Sarah crouched over him, her glowing hand on the handle.

Jacques punched her in the side of the head, and she wavered.

I did what anyone facing evil would. I called for help, but not for Puca.

Fuck that!

I was never whistling for him again. I snapped my fingers, and I called for George.

CHAPTER 27

SARAH

Mercia burst through a hole in the wall with Nick in tow. She came to a rushing stop and snapped her fingers. A teeth-rattling roar cut the air as a blast of flame covered the opening in the roof.

George's claws curled around the metal roofing, pulling it. The metal screamed in protest as he widened the opening like a tin can and stuck his head through.

"Jacques," the beast released a laughing roar, his mouth opening as he moved in.

The yawning maw angled over Jacques, and I found myself hoping the creature would eat him. Jacques shifted, and suddenly I was shoved back against a wall, along with Janice. The generator room was filled with another dragon, a silver scaled one.

Oh shit! Now there are two of them.

George had four limbs and a thin whip-like tail. He could stand on his hind legs, resembling his previous bipedal state. His gray scales shone like the gray of marble. It was smoky, rich, and smooth.

Jacques, on the other hand, had only two arms and a very long thick tail. His scales were polished silver and reflective.

My mouth dried on the reality. Jacques could kill everyone here, and I wouldn't be able to stop him. My hand went to my throat, and I tried to scream. The magic held my voice box in its spell, and the box remained silent. The rumble I could create in my belly, too, didn't rise to make a sound. The walls around me ran with my watery tears.

We are all going to die here if I can't fix this.

My fingers scratched at the skin protecting my neck, yet no amount of pain could change the magic.

Janice lay slumped next to me. His wakes faded with every beat of his heart as my chest tightened in time with him. Everywhere I looked, something wasn't right. Nick, too, carried a sickly wake of an injury. Mercia's magic colored his. She'd healed him not long ago. The girl next to Mercia, too, showed signs of drugs. She seemed familiar, but I couldn't place her.

I got to my feet, but a second later, Jacques' big tail lashed me back to the ground breaking part of a wing. "Stay down, wife! I'll be back for you." The sound was more of a rumble than Jacques' normal tone. My head hit the ground, and my eyes rolled around in my head. The weight of Jacques' tail disappeared. When my eyes finally stopped moving, the generator room was empty. Jacques was gone along with George.

The screams of battle raged in the sky. Every few moments, something heavy hit the ground and shook the building. Dust filtered down from the rafters and joined the rain to make a grimy mess.

My wing throbbed in pain, as did my head. I was sure I had a concussion. I was stuck between wanting to puke my guts out and not fall down.

Mercia was at my side, "Sarah," was all she could say. Her face told me everything I needed to know. She was scared.

If Mercia is afraid, we are all very fucked.

The girl didn't see anything other than obstacles for her to work around. Jacques was a different story, even for her.

"Janice is dying. We need to do something for him," Nick remarked. "Sarah, sing and save him."

"She can't. Jacques silenced her," Janice whispered. He coughed and groaned. I petted his face and begged with my eyes for him not to speak to save himself. My mental pleading didn't hit its mark, his eyes closed, and his breath went shallow.

I silently screamed, and my left hand ignited in flame. Fresh blood leaked from the knife wound in Janice's chest. The girl moved in to hold me. "It is okay," she whispered. "We will figure this out." My head whipped around to look at her.

How can this girl think everything would turn out alright?

Janice was dying, and there was nothing I could do. "Mercia?" the girl inquired. There was no please, or begging, only her honest wondering.

"Olive, the hunter's curse only works when you have someone to pull from. You and Nick are too weak. I need another, someone else for this to work." She shook her head.

I mouthed Olive, and my right hand gripped the girls chin and turned her face this way and that. The blond hair was still there though tipped in black. Her blue eyes were clear. The bow-shaped mouth was the same. The only difference was the womanly shape of everything.

The flame in my left hand quelled. I forced her to look at me, and I mouthed, "Zoe?"

"She's upstairs, asleep. We left her there." Olive turned to Mercia, "We could use Zoe. She's healthy."

"No way. I will not chance the loss of a child to save an adult. I have rules. Pregnant women are off-limits,"

Mercia replied, inspecting Janice's wound. "It's close to his heart. We can't move him. Another shift, and he'll bleed out. It will nick something important, and it will be over."

My head whirled with the speed of the conversation.

Zoe, here and pregnant? Olive, all grown up and fighting next to Mercia?

And then it hit me. *Bonn!* He could save Janice. The summer court had the ability to heal.

Nick moved in to stand next to Mercia. He leaned over and whispered in her ear, "We should call Puca. Whatever he's doing, this is more important."

I slapped the floor to get their attention and shook my head. NO.

"Sarah, Puca could tip the balance of this fight. We need him. If you can't sing, we need someone who has a chance of beating Jacques. George isn't alive. He's... He's an undead dragon, a zombie." Nick crossed his arms, tucking his hands under his armpits.

I flashed to him and got right in his face. Puca was on a job for me, and I needed him to finish it. No matter what happened here. I mouthed, *NO*, again, *he's working for me*.

"There were a bunch of guys at the door out front." Mercia didn't say what she was going to do, but the unfinished idea hung in the air like the smoke from the burned-out generators. I'd seen all the men around these buildings. None of them were human. They all had stolen Fae blood.

Mercia glanced at me. She'd already made her choice. I didn't know what she was waiting for. Olive touched me. I flinched away and tipped my head in agreement.

Mercia flashed out the door, heading for the front of the building with Nick close on her heels.

"Sarah, I could give you some mint to help your throat?" Olive offered. I shook my head. No amount of herbs or tea could change the magic.

A few minutes later, Mercia returned with two guys in tow and Nick covered in blood. She dumped the first guy next to Janice and laid a hand over one of his wounds.

The man began to scream, as did Janice. The blade that was in Janice's chest worked its way out at a slow pace. The guy turned into a husk of human life. His eyes sunk into his skull, and life left him just as the blade left Janice's chest. I gripped his hand with a ferocity I didn't know I had.

Mercia finished the second guy on Janice. I'd never seen anything like what just happened. Mercia was able to transfer life from one person to another. In my old life, it would have been proclaimed a miracle, or they would have killed her. One way or another, this was a curse. That level of control over life and death was dangerous.

A roar tore the air, and the side of the building crumbled as the tail of a dragon bashed it in. The silver scales told me who it was. Dragons' screams and roars surrounded us as George and Jacques fought.

"Sarah, burn the fuck out of Jacques with your hand," Nick said.

I shook my head in reply.

"She can't," Janice informed him. "A Queen cannot hurt her husband and vice versa. Jacques wants her alive so he can rule through her. The silence song is to stop her from helping anyone free her from her marriage."

Nick stared me down, "You know I must." I flashed to his side to cover his mouth, but it was too late. The whistle was out before my fingers met his lips.

The wall shivered, and Puca stepped through. Jacques roared in the background. A chunk of George landed not far from Mercia. She sniffed and nudged the mass with her boot. I expected the meat to bleed. It didn't. It smelled of rotten flesh left in the sun too long.

"Father," was all Nick said.

"What is wrong?" Puca demanded and took a few steps toward his son. The sickly pallor still clung to him. Anyone with eyes could see it.

"Sarah was silenced by Jacques, and she can't attack," was his reply.

Puca laughed and shuffled around the chunk of rotting meat in the middle of the room. "So end the marriage," he returned as if divorcing a Fae King was that easy.

Sure, I'll snap my fingers, and it will be over.

I cocked an eyebrow at him and sighed.

"You doubt me? Jillian unmade me. All you lack is a voice that I can help with." He slicked his black hair back and moved in next to me. His smile was kind and quiet, not the triumphant ego ride he normally sported.

Puca sang,

"When the pie was opened,

All the birds began to sing,

Wasn't that a tasty dish to set before the Queen?"

The tension in my throat vanished, and I replied, "Is it done?" The thank-you would never pass my lips. Instead, my one burning question crowded its way to the forefront.

His smile changed to one of knowing, "Almost, I have one last thing to do, and then we are ready. Keep Mercia alive," he whispered. "Now go unmake your King." He ripped his portal and left to a meadow where the sun was just peeking over the moss-green hills. Behind him lay the stones. Just as quickly, the portal closed.

I didn't wait another second. I flashed past the crumbled wall to stand in the rain as two dragons battled overhead. "Jacques, your wife calls you to her side," I yelled, pushing as much compulsion into my call as my body possessed.

Dragon Jacques crashed to the ground in front of me with George's neck gripped in his mouth. Blood leaked out around razor-sharp teeth. George was weak and missing more flesh than the one piece I'd seen.

Jacques released George and spit his curdled blue blood out. "Wife," he chuckled.

"I divorce you. You are no longer my King and husband. I take the magic back."

Jacques shifted on my last word. His form was one of a Fae, and his silvery eyes burned into me. I sang for a shield a moment before he hummed for control of a pet.

Mercia rushed to my side and snapped her fingers. "You can't steal what's mine!" She shouted. The fear from before was wiped away with the thrill of the hunt, and it was contagious. The taste of the hunt was thick in the air. I savored the flavor. I needed it to energize my drive to kill. Because kill, I would.

"Pil's child, we finally meet. Come to me. I am your grandfather and rightful master." He held out his hand.

"You must think my head is full of pixie shit to believe anything you say. I already have one master I don't want, and it isn't you," Mercia replied with a laugh. "This is the part where he tries to explain why I should join him, yadda, yadda."

I burst out laughing. I didn't know anyone knew what yadda, yadda meant anymore. Janice took his place at my back, and Nick joined Mercia at her side. Olive stayed close to the building.

"Olive, go get Zoe," I ordered.

Jacques threw a few cheap songs at us; they were to test and soften us up. Jacques opened a portal in front of

Olive. I hummed for a shield to block her from entering the portal to where ever Jacques planned on sending her.

"You will not take my people," I shouted. My elemental hand lit with my anger.

"You may be able to stop me now, Sarinha, but I always win," he laughed and tossed a few weak-ass songs in my direction. He shifted to a wolf and leaped at me. The deep growl in his chest waked at me. Over salivating teeth, he ground out, "Queens don't shift." His mouth moved to bite down as his feet pushed me in the chest, slamming me to the ground.

Janice pounded his fist into the wolf's head. A second later, not one but two wolves jumped on Jacques and began tearing at his limbs. Their jaws snapped and ripped at his flesh. Jacques shifted back to his Fae form and sang a huntsman's tail of killing wolves.

The wakes formed and raced for Nick and Mercia. I plucked them from the air and twisted them around my fingers, re-knitting them into the jungle book story of wolves helping people survive. Mercia shifted back and sang for sixpence. Weakness was lining her every move.

We were all tired.

As I racked my brain for a return to his next attack, the ring on my right-hand beat in time with my heart's desire. The red stone was the only way.

CHAPTER 28

MERCIA

Sarah changed the magic from a death blow to some kid named Mowgli. Nick chuckled and leaped away from a Jack song Jacques threw at us.

I sang to drop part of the house that Jack built on his head. Instead of chunks of cement falling on his head, the spell fell flat.

"You can't use my spells against me. I would have thought Pil taught you that," he laughed at me.

My nostrils flared.

How dare he laugh at what Momma overlooked?

I'd learned a lot of new songs after Momma, magic that didn't involve Jacques.

Sarah lifted her right hand; it carried the red stone ring. All my bravado bled away to be replaced with fear.

"I don't need to beat you, only take back the magic," she stated. Her broken wing fluttered and lay still as she winched. The wakes around the red stone grew. The fighting in the distance, too, came to a standstill. The world seemed to hold its breath as everything moved slower than it should.

I pulled the crossbow off the ground and aimed it at Jacques. Sarah's ring struck like a viper. I knew that pain. The magic locked its fangs into Jacques sucking his power away.

Jacques' cries of agony filled the air and my heart.

Momma is truly free now.

The silvery wakes around him turned from the dark of the autumn court to a white, as if all the deeds of his life were nothing more than poison to be removed. His white hair changed to a simple platinum blond, shimmering in the early morning light.

"You are no longer a Prince or a one-time King. You are a lowly Fae, no better than a kitchen worker. Danu made you her son to share her life. Instead, you stole it away from her. Your mother! You killed her for a pernicious woman's ambitions. Shame on you!" Sarah was crying, her tears flowing freely.

From far off in the distance came Nick's sword. Sarah put her hand up and grabbed it out of the sky. Then, in one swift move, she sliced Jacque's head off.

It fell through the air to land next to what was left of George. His one good eye latched on to the rolling skull. Quick as a wink, he swallowed it whole. George lumbered to his feet and took the few steps necessary to reach Jacques' body and devoured that too. After that, he sat down, heaved a sigh, and looked at me, "Master, release me so I may rejoin the magic. I have no need to continue this existence."

I moved to his side. "A hunter doesn't keep its kill in pain longer than they should. I release you from my service and life." I laid my hand over one of his wounds and pulled the dead life from him. It was a horrible rotting flavor of entrails left in the sun too long. My belly rolled over, and I gagged as the dead energy filtered from one hand to the ground where the blood of the dead belongs.

Terra would use it to feed the next season. Aer would dry it out, and Aqualis would wash it away.

Sarah's left hand burned what was left of George's body. The fire of Fae was no match for an elemental's flames. The raging white flames turned George into dust within moments.

As the ashy outline of his form disappeared, I whispered, *thank you*. I glanced around to see if anyone had heard me.

None save Nick.

He grabbed my hand and gave it a squeeze, then pulled the back of my hand to his lips and kissed it.

Olive appeared with her sister at her side. She smiled as Zoe burst into tears at the sight of Sarah. For a moment, I thought they were going to squeal like pigs and hug one another. But they didn't.

"You kept your word," was all Zoe said. Sarah tipped her head to her and ripped a portal into the air, "All those with Fae blood," she pointed and said nothing more. The compulsion of the Queen didn't draw me to the portal, not more than what would come next.

I'd seen what Puca was up to. I had two jobs left to really be free from all my oaths.

Danu, help me!

I didn't know if I could do what had to be done. These were the only tasks that mattered after saving Nick. The Fae-human war had to end, and I had the only means to end it.

I quivered as I stepped through to the meadow in Ireland. It was where it all began. There, I saw the stone circle in its full glory with Puca standing guard nearby.

CHAPTER 29

SARAH

Life always comes full circle.

Just thinking about that statement made me laugh. It was probably Fae in origin.

I shook my head to remove the wanderings of my tired mind. It was time, yet I wasn't ready. I gazed around at the small gathering of what was left of Fae, whether full or part. There couldn't be more than a few hundred. Many were covered in dust and grime. Their faces were scratched with limbs hanging at odd angles. Their clothes were soaked with blood. The evidence of our hard-won victory lined every face. My chest tightened on the knowledge of how many had died. It only drove home to me the rightness of this choice.

I changed my stance and pulled my body to its full height. My chest expanded as I sucked in air, ready to order Mercia to give me the song —

"I said I would never leave you alone in these Hallowed Hills," Nick stated, his soft green eyes turned into hard jade. "Take them and go," he said before he began singing.

A scream ripped from Mercia's throat, "Nooo!" She beat his chest with her fist. He only wrapped an arm around her waist and pulled her in tight. "You can't," she screamed, then blubbered something about not telling him the song.

The stone circle next to me released a sonic boom, blasting everyone to the ground. I leaped to my feet to stand next to the waking mouth of the stone circle and the wormhole it created.

The vision on the other side was a mirror of what earth once was with a heavy green hue. It was an earth I'd never seen. It resembled paintings from the past. An impressionist could not have given you a more idyllic vision. The magic softened the edges giving the other world a dream-like quality.

The dusty golden light rimmed the mountain range in the distance, and I longed to climb those mountains. I wanted to see this other world from the top down. My one good wing twitched with the desire to take me there.

Nick winked at me, and his voice continued on in the background, reminding me that the portal would only last as long as his song. He would never pass through the stones, he was the anchor, and this was our one chance.

Changing gears, I whirled around to take in my subjects. "If you wish to remain Fae, walk through the stones of Danu. Anyone not entering the stones will either die or become human. Choose your destiny."

There was an initial rush of bodies, each wanting to ensure their continued existence. They moved like a herd with wolves at their heels, desperate to reach the safety of the portal and the world beyond. My only hope was the portal wasn't a cliff that I was running my people over.

My mother stopped in front of me, still holding the hand of the boy I'd sent her to watch over. "I won't be going with you," she stated, her blue eyes watered with unshed tears. "I'm not like you, Sarah. I can't live the life of a Fae. I'm not human either. I'm something else, and I must stay here. It's where I belong." Her lower lip trembled, and she petted the hair on the boy's head.

I wanted to pull a song from my heart and push her through the portal, to force her to stay with me. I should have made Arty stay. He would be alive right now if I had.

I chose wrong then. I won't let that happen again.

Her lips pulled back into a sad smile. "If you force me to go, you'll end up hating yourself. You were right to let Arthur go." She squeezed my shoulder.

I shook my head to deny the truth. "I can't let you," I whispered.

More Fae rushed past, some jumping through the waking circle, others stepping into the magic like it was a stream of water.

"Yes, you can. I have only stayed for you. I promised Father I would care for you, and I have. My job as keeper is over."

"You stopped being keeper when you gave Pil the stone bowl," I scoffed and shook my head.

"That is not what being keeper meant." She pushed my hair out of my eyes, "We were the keepers of the child of Danu. Our job was to keep you safe until you emerged from your chrysalis. Our work is done." She kissed my cheek. "Now pull the magic from me. I no longer want or need it. The only thing I want is for you to promise me you'll dream of impossible things and think of me."

"I thought Cernunnos was my father."

"No, Puca is, as Danu is your mother." She glanced behind me.

I turned to find Puca. His devil may care attitude was gone. He looked from mom to me and back. "Alice, you can still go with us. Magic or not."

"No, Father, even Demelza knew we didn't belong in Fae. I will stay." She hugged the boy to her. She was staying for him. My mother needed to be needed. The boy was human, and that was why she stayed.

If I hugged her, I might break.

My blood ties to Puca and Danu didn't mean anything to me. They weren't my parents and never would be.

I'd always believed my mom was weak. That she would crumble under pressure.

I've misread everything in my life.

"I love you," was all I could say.

The red ring weighed heavy on my hand as I raised it to wield the magic. I closed my eyes. I didn't want to watch the shadowed Fae marking that lined my mother's skin disappear. I didn't want to see her scream in agony as the magic was forcibly sucked from her. She chose this, and I couldn't deny her a choice I never had.

I would not have chosen Fae.

"I love you too," she replied.

"Stop!" Cernunnos shouted. "Alice,"

The hungry magic struck, and mom screamed in time with the stones' pull. Each draw pulled a little more, working like a throat gulping the magic down as it swallowed.

A hard blow rammed into my side, and my eyes flew open.

"Stop!" Mom shouted as Cernunnos wrapped an arm around the boy and drug him through the portal, disappearing in the wakes. Mom took one look at me, shrugged, and leaped through the stones after them.

"What the fuck just happened?" I demanded.

Puca burst into laughter. He bent over and slapped his thigh. "Alice was never going to get rid of that Fae no matter what she did. A hunter will not be denied his prey."

I glared at him. "What about what she wanted?"

"Sarinha, let it be. Alice will be happy. She was before. She only left Fae because of you. Trust me."

I expected him to say something or hug me. To make some proclamation of parenthood. He harried Nick enough times about it. He didn't. Instead, he stood next to me as more Fae moved into the portal. Gone was the tapping, shuffling, and dancing, the nervous ticks I'd always associated with Puca.

Was it all a lie? Is this the real Puca?

Changelings came and went. A few asked to be turned, and I pulled the magic from their bones. But most just wanted Fae. They moved through the portal to the other side. A few knelt down before me and lowered their heads while crossing their left arm over their chest.

"Please," was all they said.

I didn't need more. No Fae would ever beg. The simple human plea was enough. Their choice was made, and the ring devoured their magic with its hungry heart. Their screams filled the air, tearing at my psyche.

When it was over, their bodies slumped to the ground. Other humans came and carried them away. Fear lined the faces of all.

The crowd disappeared, leaving only Janice, Puca, Nick, Mercia, and I.

"Nick will never leave," Puca said. He nodded his head and moved to stand next to him.

"I need you," I stopped. That very human *please* could not escape my lips. "I need your counsel, " I gulped back everything else that I wanted to say.

"Until the balance is returned, I must stay," Puca shrugged.

"I don't understand," I looked around, hoping someone else would have the answer. They were just as confused as I was. "I thought killing Jacques was the solution," I groaned.

"No. He was the cause, not the solution. No. The magic screams in agony as if it's divided. It's not whole but being pulled apart. It must be restored, and I must stay until that is so."

Nick's voice wavered as he grew tired. The wakes in the stone circle flickered.

"Sarah, we must go," Janice murmured.

I nodded in understanding. I moved to Nick and wrapped my arms around him. "Thank you," I whispered and placed a kiss on his cheek. He winked back at me but continued singing.

I thrust my hand out to Mercia. She eyed it warily, then took it. Nestled in my palm was the red stone ring. "Use it with care. I owe you a boon."

Her blue eyes twinkled with a wicked light. "Don't worry, I'll clean up after you." She took the ring and slipped it into her left hand.

Janice led me to the portal and stepped through, still holding my hand. As I moved to enter, my body stopped at the magic wall. Janice was on the other side. I hammered my hands into the wakes, but they wouldn't let me through.

My left hand glowed with the elemental fire, and I screamed. "No!"

I whirled around to stare Puca down. "Why, why can't I pass?"

An oily voice flowed over my senses, "Because you are tied to this world. You are one of the elements. I did not make them. They were already here. You must stay." The cloaked figure of the record keeper stood at the tree line.

"You didn't make anything. Only Danu was here at the beginning of time. I will not suffer your dilutions. Pass through the portal or die!" Puca shouted.

The creature moved to join our circle. Its spider-like fingers curled around the hood covering its face and pulled the black fabric back to reveal a beautifully twisted face with a jagged scar covering most of her face and neck.

Puca gasped, "My love," he fell at her feet and began kissing her hands.

"I am no longer Danu. I cannot sing," the woman informed us.

"Why did you not come to me? I would have healed you. You could sing again. None of this would have happened," Puca said, rubbing the side of his face into her hands.

"My last act of magic was to save our child. I never wanted to be a Queen or rule. I never dreamed that my Fae children would turn on me. But that is all in the past. I will go back to my world. I should never have left. I am the cause of all of this. My thirst for knowledge and power." She shook her head.

Hubris is a sin many fall prey to.

I wilted. The knowledge that I couldn't pass seeped into my bones, and I sank to my knees. Agony tore at my insides. All those tears I bottled up found their way to my eyes. I released them to run down my face and neck into my clothes. Sweat formed on my forehead as the magic in my belly began to grow. I didn't care about Danu or balance in magic. I didn't even care that they did all of this to save me. My head turned of its own volition to stare through the portal. On the other side were Janice and mom.

And I am here. I will always be here.

I couldn't be human because I never was.

My hand glowed with power, and I cursed the day I killed Ignis. She tricked me into killing her, knowing I could never leave. She knew about the portal.

Of course, she knew,

They are made of stone. I screeched in anger.

"Why save me for all of this?" I demanded and stared the one-time King and Queen down." My hand burst into flame, and I took to my feet. "Take it back! Take it all back. I never wanted any of this!" I shouted.

Nick's voice wavered.

I looked from Puca to Danu. I pointed at the stone circle, "Go! Your people need you. I don't and never did. I would have been better off without you!" I screamed.

Puca's shoulders straightened, and he stepped through the wakes. For once, he didn't say a fucking thing. Danu, however, didn't go. She looked from Mercia to me and back.

"Someone must stay to control the Hallowed Hills, hunter," she stated. Mercia tilted her head down and crossed her arm over her chest, and with crossed fingers, she touched her forehead.

I ignored her act of obedience to Danu. I was used to her denying me. She was one of the few that could. "Don't worry, we will take care of what's left," I growled.

"The balance must be restored," Danu stated.

Mercia flashed in front of me, "Yes, my Queen," and she sliced my abdomen open.

CHAPTER 30

SARAH

My blade cut into Sarah's belly like the gelatinous goo left over from a pot that had cooked too long and cooled. Her ropy guts peeked out as blood poured from the gash. The hunter in me wanted to let her die. She wasn't my Queen. She was a pretender. My human side choked on what I had to do. She was my friend, sort of, and I hesitated.

Sarah's eyes lit with the shock of my attack. Behind the shock was a deep hurt. One that flavored the air. It was anis and cream of tartar. I glanced at Danu, and she tilted her head. This was the only way.

I thrust my hand into the hot bloody mass that contained Sarah's organs and began to sing her life away. The hunter's curse was a sticky sweet drug I could get lost in. If the other were a drink, this was a cosmic ocean of power. A Queen carried the power of creation in her blood, and I needed to concentrate and find the solution to this problem. There, in her blood, was the magic that didn't belong. Her power over fire and that part that made her Queen.

I dug through all the magic strands that made Sarah who she was and pulled them apart. The hunter portion of her came from Puca, which was really more wyld predator than a hunter. She, like Puca, was a shifter and could mimic other things.

Elemental fire was only embedded in her left hand and easy to detangle and suck out. And suck, I did. The fire tasted of the root of a mellow marsh and sugar. The tang of a volcano peppered the magic, creating a skin over the entire mass. I devoured the burning clump. As I pulled the magic free from her body and mine grew warm.

The hand I had buried in her glowed with the element I now controlled. My eyes lit with new magic, and the darkness was pushed back even further than my Fae sight had provided.

That left only the power of a Queen to pull out.

The heat in new my fiery hand was cauterizing the wound, and the blood flow ceased. I pulled it free with a sick gushing sound. The internal organs I left behind were partially cooked, making the gash in her belly smoke.

"You fucking bitch!" She spat a moment before her hand crashed into the side of my head, and I careened toward the portal. My hands caught the side stones and dug my fingers in to stop the forward momentum before I was lost to the other world. I glanced over my shoulder to see Sarah and her dripping gut wound flashing toward me as she sang to stitch it closed. I cartwheeled sideways and pivoted around Danu, putting her between myself and the portal.

"There can be only one Queen. That is the imbalance," I replied, then faked a dodge left and moved right. She beat me there.

"If that's true, then why didn't Puca figure it out?" She shouted. Sarah was letting her emotions run away with her, and when creatures run, I chase.

"He was too blinded by his quest to fix everything to see the simple solution. One Queen has to die and stay dead," I shrugged.

"Oh, and you and Dusty over there get to decide? Hun?" she asked, hooking a thumb at Danu.

"No, the magic gets to do that. And it did, thousands of years ago, when Danu lived, but the other Queens kept dying. Now let me finish," I replied. A smile crept over my face, pulling my lips tight, revealing my fresh canines. The rush of a change moved over me, and my paws found the dirt. I dug my claws in and leaped at her. But she sang *who let the dogs out*, and I landed on my side on the ground with a shield holding me in place.

I transformed back to my Fae shape and opened a portal under me, slipping through the magical opening away from the stone circle, only to roll up onto my feet.

"I've seen what you do with your hunter's curse. I'm not a Slurpee!" She shouted and began to sing a song to lock me up.

I pulled the trigger on my crossbow, and the bolt lodged in her back next to her spine. Her arms raised into the air as she fell to her knees at my feet. She blinked up at me. "I thought we were friends."

I quickly turned her face down and pulled the bolt from her back, laid my right hand over the weeping hole, and dug a finger in, "Magic has no friends, and oaths don't care about feeling." I began to pull. The Queen's magic was wrapped around her heart like an octopus. Each tentacle dug in deep and ready to rip her apart to keep its power.

Now I understood why the red stone was so important. A hunter's curse could never suck the magic out, only the stone. I would only take her life if I continued.

I pulled my finger from the wound and burned it closed with my fiery left hand. She screeched as she arched in pain. I closed my right fist and pointed the red stone at her.

"I am sorry, Sarah. It is the only way." The human words tasted bitter on my tongue. I knew them to be true. I was sorry. I blinked back the emotions threatening me.

Magic can heal or kill.

Sometimes it only makes you wish for death.

The magic of the ring pulled at her, and she screamed in agony as her Fae side ripped free. Her thorny crown melted back into her head. The mark of Fae that decorated her body faded away, and her wings withered and dried before breaking off.

The hole in her back began to bleed again, but I kept going. She turned on to her side and curled up as babies do, holding her legs tight to her chest. She whimpered and screamed until finally, she looked as Fae as I did.

She was no longer Queen. The power to rule was no longer hers to wield. I pulled the ring from my hand and laid it on the ground at Danu's feet. I knelt and tilted my head up to take in the Queen I'd chosen.

"Are you happy?" I shouted, "She was my one friend, and you ruined it. Can I be free now?" The heat in my left hand scorched the earth where it touched with a power I never wanted.

"Yes, you are free," she replied. The emotion I expected to come from those words never reached her eyes or her wakes. She was cold and stoic. The long centuries of waiting killed off those feeling, leaving on the chill of the Queen.

Nick was still singing in the background, and I took to my feet to join him.

The magic ties locked around me loosed and fell away only to disappear. I was free for the first time since Momma died. There was no joy in this freedom. Sarah lay on her side, covered in sweat. Her wounds leaked blood onto the ground, and small mushrooms formed around her.

Nick pulled me into the crook of his shoulder. I patted his arm and stepped away. Hunters don't feel regret over a kill.

Fae don't cry for a fallen foe.

Tears wanted to escape me and mourn the loss of my friend. Sarah peeked one eye open and sneered at me.

Danu picked up the stone, put it on her finger, and transformed. Her neck healed in an instant, wings burst from her back the golden color of a daisy's heart. Her crown grew to an epic proportion, and it was the same shade of yellow as her wings.

The sheer beauty that made Danu burst in my breast. I wanted to cry for a joy I'd never encountered. She smiled at me, and I returned it eagerly.

She turned her attention to Sarah, and a song emanated from her as sweet as any ocean wave or a bird's tune. Sarah's body convulsed as the hole in her back and gash in her belly closed. The broken skin around her face and across her arms became smooth. Then Danu snapped her fingers, clearing all the grim and blood away.

Sarah's eyes peeked open, "You should have killed me," she stated.

"I didn't want to, but I would have if the magic demanded it," I remarked.

Danu hummed, '*come back, Peter, come back, Paul.*' Sarah's body lifted into the air. Danu thrust her into the stone circle, tossed the ring back at me, and flew in behind her.

I caught the ring and choked on my feelings. Nick's voice stopped.

The stone circle died behind us. Its stones were inert as if they never worked at all. I slumped to the ground and let my human side take over. I cried.

Nick held me for a long while. I think he cried too. But I was too involved with my own tears to be sure. When I finally came to my senses, the sun touched the horizon.

"How did you know what to sing? I never told you." I asked.

"I peeked in the bag while I was in the tower. Pil wasn't there, and Arty promised not to tell. It was easy to see the song in the center was different from the rest. All I had was time. Anyway, it wasn't until Puca told me we were looking for a song that I knew what I'd seen," he shrugged and kissed my forehead.

"Why didn't you say something?" I demanded. And shoved his shoulder.

"You were mad at me. I didn't get the chance. But hey, you found a zombie dragon. I know a ton of people that would worship you for just that. Or I did," he remarked. The smile on his face faded away.

"What do we do now?" I asked, then sniffled.

Crying makes your nose run. Yuck.

"We make sure there are no Fae left on the surface. Humanity will forget after a while, and this time they will never have a reason to remember that fairies existed." Nick kissed my neck and pulled me deeper into his arms.

"That's not what I meant. What about us? What do we do?" I turned my head to look at Nick.

A wicked gleam hit his eyes, "We fuck like rabbits?" He kissed my neck and then took a bite.

"We can't have kids. They would be Fae," I pointed out. The thought saddened me. I never thought of becoming a mother.

Though I never had Nick before either.

"We have the ring. We pull the Fae from them." He sniffled into my hair, mimicking a dog.

I scrunched my nose at the idea.

"We keep them in the wilds and teach them control. What else can we do?"

I liked Nick's solution. It was simple and clean.

The stone circle was proof that Fae once existed here. I pointed the finger at the stones and wiggled the tip.

"What? Do you want me to solve everything?" he groaned.

I got up and pulled the wand from the capstone. I placed it on the ground and crushed it under my heel. I never wanted anyone to use the stones again. Our two worlds didn't belong together. We could never live in peace. Fae would trick and toy while humans would steal and abuse, each killing the other along the way.

"Do you think Sarah will forgive me?" I asked.

"You gave her everything she wanted. She's no longer Queen, she can live in peace, and she has Janice. I think she will get over it as soon as she gets over the fact you kicked her ass," he chuckled.

"So that's a no."

"Yep, no. But she is there, and you are here." He nuzzled my neck and sniffed.

I wanted to wiggle away. I probably smelled like a street rat. "You chose me over her?" I smiled at him.

"That was an easy choice. I love Sarah, but I'm not in love with her. That part of me is solely owned by you." He leaned down and kissed me. "Can we fuck like rabbits now?"

"Yes, yes, we can." My lips met his, and the fucked-up world around us disappeared.

The end

TECHNO WITCH

Witch craft has been hidden and feared for all of human history with good reason.

If you've enjoyed what you've read here please give it a little love and leave a review and feel free to follow me on Amazon Or follow me on Instagram @s.l.mason_author

KILLING GODS

ALETHEA

We are not Gods. No matter what Zeus thinks.

Herathina

Log Entry ATD 1,784,652.51 Terra

The study of evolution had come to a standstill when we discovered Terra. It was the perfect incubator for a Millennial Project. But from the beginning, everything has gone wrong.

Our mandate said limited contact, not domination but Poseidon is too blinded by his lust for that human to listen.

Sydney

present day

My dreams are filled with an island of blue and a woman's indiscernible pleas. On the back of the dreams come abilities. Abilities I'm desperate to hide.

But it's the voice, in my mind that terrifies me most. Is it real or have I cracked? Can you live a normal life if you aren't?

Where is the island, who is the voice in my mind, what does the woman want, and how do I hide the truth and still appear normal on the outside?